She stood there, hands on hips and blue eyes flaring. Magnificent.

Her whole body radiated unleashed energy. He'd foolishly indulged himself with that one kiss as a spur of the moment thing. But he hadn't been able to help himself. Her face had been flushed from running, her chest heaving, and his mind had gone blank. The draw of her lips had been a magnet pulling on his libido.

His mind was perfectly clear now. She was in danger, and yet all he wanted to do was kiss her again. To lose himself in the depths of her rosy mouth and soft body.

He dug his fingers through his hair. "Rylie, listen to me, please." His own voice was thick with need and shook with fear—for her. "I'm trying to save your life. I could be walking into a trap. The Taj Zabbar..." What could he say to make her understand that all he wanted was her safety?

Dear Reader,

When I was a little girl, I loved getting lost in the fantasies between the pages of a book. Some of my favorite stories were the tales of the Arabian nights. As a teenager, one of my favorite movie themes centered on a dark sheik coming to the rescue of the fair maiden and the two of them riding across the desert into the sunset.

In my new DESERT SONS series, a new world threat has appeared out of the stark deserts and oases of an ancient land. An old enemy with new wealth has gained power and begins a covert war of retribution.

In the first book, *Her Sheik Protector*, the oldest Kadir brother, Darin, comes face-to-face with his own desperate obsession for love as he fights for his family. He finds his true love—just as she becomes the target for revenge.

Come along with me and ride into the mists of an ancient tale. Let's get lost in the story together.

Happy reading,

Linda

LINDA
CONRAD

Her Sheik Protector

ROMANTIC
SUSPENSE

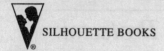

SILHOUETTE BOOKS

ISBN-13: 978-0-373-27688-2

HER SHEIK PROTECTOR

Copyright © 2010 by Linda Lucas Sankpill

This edition published by arrangement with Harlequin Books S.A.

For questions and comments about the quality of this book please contact us at Customer_eCare@Harlequin.ca.

® and TM are trademarks of Harlequin Books S.A., used under license. Trademarks indicated with ® are registered in the United States Patent and Trademark Office, the Canadian Trade Marks Office and in other countries.

Visit Silhouette Books at www.eHarlequin.com

Printed in U.S.A.

Books by Linda Conrad

LINDA CONRAD

When asked about her favorite things, Linda Conrad lists a longtime love affair with her husband, her sweetheart of a dog named KiKi and a sunny afternoon with nothing to do but read a good book. Inspired by generations of storytellers in her family and pleased to have many happy readers' comments, Linda continues creating her own sensuous and suspenseful stories about compelling characters finding love.

A bestselling author of more than twenty-five books, Linda has received numerous industry awards, among them the National Reader's Choice Award, the Maggie, the Write Touch Readers' Award and the *RT Book Reviews* Reviewers' Choice Award. To contact Linda, read more about her books or to sign up for her newsletter and/or contests, go to her Web site at www.LindaConrad.com.

To Jo Ann Zimmerman, who lived one of the most romantic stories of two people meeting that I have ever read. Thanks for your story!

And to the amazing author and my dear friend Karen Kendall. A special thanks for solving the mystery for me. You're the greatest!

Prologue

Running late.

Rylie Hunt knew it was her own danged fault she wouldn't be on time for the presentation. She'd foolishly told her father she wasn't coming at all and then stormed off in a huff. Oh, Lordy, how would she ever make it up to him?

Finally locating a remote spot to park, she shut down the engine of her snazzy red Corvette. The parking lot of her family's newest oil-and-gas shipping facility was packed to overflowing due to the grand-opening celebration. The grand-opening celebration that her father, CEO of Hunt Drilling, had originally intended for her to officiate at as the vice president.

The mere idea of disappointing her dad gave her a sad twinge. Everyone had always said she was "Daddy's little girl with an attitude." But their last argument had been too bitter and had gone way too far. She and Marshall "Red" Hunt were too much alike—even down to their auburn hair. They butted heads on nearly every subject. Today she was making herself crazy wild, worrying over exactly how mad her dad would be this time.

If she hadn't been late, Rylie would've stopped by the restaurant where she knew her mother was setting things up for the new board of directors' luncheon. Her mother could give her a clue as to Daddy's state of mind and to his reactions over the rather childish way she'd acted yesterday. With a wistful sigh, she prayed that her mom the peacemaker had already smoothed over this latest problem caused by Rylie's big fat mouth.

But she was running late and she hadn't taken the time to find out. She'd landed her little Diamond DA42 Twin Star at Executive Airport. Then she'd jumped into her car and raced toward the Houston Ship Channel, heading for the grand-opening celebration and her father. Eager to apologize, she couldn't wait to get this test of their normally loving relationship behind them.

After locking her car, she planted her feet on the hot and sticky surface of the asphalt parking lot. She jammed the keys into her jeans pocket, refusing to pay any heed to the weird vibes she was suddenly getting. Okay, maybe deep in her subconscious she knew something—somewhere—wasn't quite right.

The creepy sensation of being watched crawled down her arms, despite her attempts to shake it off. But Rylie was too late for the ceremony to pay attention. She made herself believe that the odd sensations were due only to guilt over the stupid argument with her father. Instead of looking for more trouble, she raced toward her family's new shipping facility and the big celebration.

Daddy was bound to forgive her. She hoped.

The heat off the asphalt rose around her in waves as she weaved through the massive lot full of cars. It seemed as if she'd had to park a mile away today. Every news team in the state must've turned out for this shindig.

I'm sorry, Daddy. You were right.

Well, half-right, anyway. Despite her many misgivings about Hunt Drilling taking on new partners, partners by the name of Kadir who owned a huge international conglomerate that included the biggest shipping line in the world, her father had been positive that this move would assure continued success for their firm.

Rylie hadn't given a rip about the Kadirs' power or money. She was more worried about the public relations aspect of a Texas company going into business with a Middle Eastern–based concern. Ever since 9/11, Americans in general had been highly suspicious of even the merest hint that terrorist-influenced groups were taking over U.S. enterprises. Congress had already blocked several attempts by Middle Eastern businesses to buy American companies or real estate, and especially the port facilities.

Given enough time, Rylie was sure she could've found another company to come to Hunt's aid, though she was well aware that few shipping firms flew an American flag these days.

Her dad remained firmly convinced he was right. He'd done his homework. The Kadirs were Bedouin, he'd said. For thousands of years they'd been nomads. Not connected to any politics, religion or particular country. They were definitely not terrorists or connected to terrorism in any sense, and they could do so much to promote Hunt Drilling.

Okay, Daddy, I've thought it over and agree. The PR might still be tricky, but you win. I agree the Kadirs aren't terrorists and we'll find a way to win over the hearts of Americans with the right media. She'd given up her stubborn stand, but hoped her father wouldn't rub it in. If she had been the one who'd won, she would have gloated, and her daddy knew that well. Chuckling, she remembered how he'd always claimed she'd given him his prematurely gray hair.

In her haste to pick up the pace and make up time, Rylie stumbled over a gravel rock and went down on her knees. Shoot!

She was up on her feet again in an instant, but then decided she should stop long enough to dust off her jeans. Bending over to brush at the worst of the gravel, she thought about how glad she was to be wearing her boots and denim today instead of a fancy pantsuit or even a dress. She'd considered changing, but...

At that moment, without any warning, the whole world came apart in a powerful cataclysm. Violent gusts of wind knocked Rylie down, putting her flat on her back and taking the breath from her lungs. A flash of heat rolled over her body, singeing uncovered skin. The back of her head banged hard against the pavement, while earsplitting explosions blew out her eardrums and turned everything eerily silent.

Mustering all her physical resources, Rylie lifted her head and looked around. Through a bleary haze she saw thick, black smoke and fire, rising over her like a towering volcano a hundred feet in the air. The smell of sulphur assaulted her nose.

Dazed and confused as she was, it took a moment to understand what she was seeing. The new shipping facility was gone. All gone.

That must mean… But what had happened to her coworkers and the local reporters? What had happened to the Kadir company officials and their guests?

Light-headed and suddenly sick to her stomach, Rylie closed her eyes and slowly formed the most important question yet. What had happened to the CEO of Hunt Drilling? Where in God's name was her father?

But before her wounded brain could even start processing those answers, reality began sinking away as everything in her immediate world turned from bruised purple to soggy gray—and in seconds went completely black.

Chapter 1

Six months later

"You don't have to do this, brother. Our cousins Ben and Karim are available and prepared. It would be best to let one of them attend the conference."

Darin Kadir listened over his shoulder to his brother but concentrated on readying himself for his first mission for the family. While Shakir argued his point from the other side of the room, Darin checked the cylinder on his Ruger SP101 .357 magnum. Hefting the small double-action weapon, he felt the weight of it like ten tons of responsibility.

Sighting down the satin-finished barrel but making sure to keep his finger off the trigger, Darin answered, "My job makes me the best one for this mission. After everything that's happened, I'm still considered the vice president of Kadir Shipping. It would've been my duty to attend the annual World Industry and Shipping conference before Uncle Sunnar was killed, and it might start rumors throughout the industry if someone else went in my place."

Shakir moved around the hotel suite, stopping to stand with his back to the balcony's glass doors, still not ready to concede. "If Uncle Sunnar hadn't died in that explosion in America, you would be preparing to take over as president of the shipping division upon his retirement. But things have changed—drastically. You're not ready for a field mission for the family, Darin. We need you at headquarters, strategizing and planning."

Darin finally glanced over at his younger brother, dressed in camo fatigues and silhouetted against the stunning views of Lake Geneva and beyond to the Swiss Alps. "And let my brothers and cousins have all the fun?"

The look of sober dismay on Shakir's face was a reflection of Darin's own feelings. He pocketed the Ruger and put a steadying hand on his brother's shoulder.

"We don't know for sure if the Taj Zabbar family will send a representative to the conference." He locked his gaze with Shakir's and forced him to pay attention. "If they don't, then I'm the best one to seek out information about them from our competitors in the industry. Remember, I've been working in the shipping world for the past ten years. I know the people who come to these conferences. No one else would have their confidence the way I do."

Shakir dropped his gaze to stare at the floor, but Darin did not release the firm grip he held on his younger brother's shoulder. He remembered a time when Shakir wouldn't have questioned his big brother's decisions, though Darin had only been a couple years older. In fact for much of his life, Darin had been the father figure for his two younger brothers. At the time of their mother's death, Shakir, a ten-year-old stutterer and in particular need of help, had depended on his brother for lessons on how to develop the intense loyalty of the Kadir clan.

"I'm proud of you and Tarik," Darin told Shakir gently. "Proud of the way you both have stepped up to the challenges our family must face. I'm aware you two have far more experience in the field than I do. But that doesn't mean I can't be of service to the family by obtaining covert information."

Tarik and Shakir had both spent their adult lives in military training, Shakir for the English paratroopers and Tarik for the American Special Forces. Neither had been interested in entering the family businesses after college. Unlike Darin, who'd been eager to climb the ranks of the family's shipping company after receiving his master's degree in business at Columbia University.

But despite his business ambitions, Darin had spent the six months since the explosion secretly mastering the darker arts of weaponry and self-defense. Their father had not yet called upon him to take the lead in forming the family's new offensive line against their ancient enemy, but Darin wanted to be ready.

He thought back to right after the explosion. Ignoring their grief over losing one of their own, his father and the other elders of the Kadir clan spent considerable time debating whether the incident could have been a first volley in an undeclared war. No one had taken responsibility for the explosion, but the centuries-old legends of the Kadir–Taj Zabbar family feud were recalled and retold by the Kadirs. Recent changes in the status of the Taj Zabbar family's financial and political positions were studied in detail. Internet gossip was combed through. Then, and only then, had the Kadirs slowly conceded the possibility of the worst.

Shakir slipped out from under Darin's hand. "You take our old legends too seriously, brother. Yes, the elders have decided not to promote you to president of the shipping line yet—for fear of repercussions or another attack. But this is the twenty-first century...not the sixteenth. You can't seriously believe the Taj Zabbar might want to destroy our entire clan for something that happened between the two families centuries ago?"

"No, of course I don't." Darin straightened his tie and practically stood at attention. "But we can't overlook the possibility that when the Kadir family sided with the country of Kasht fifty years ago at the time of the first Taj Zabbar uprising, we cemented our position as their sworn enemies."

"But Kasht gave us the shipping rights and port facilities in Taj Zabbar territory that allowed our family business to rise to global dominance in three short decades." Shakir held his hands out, palms up. "The Taj Zabbar would never have let us in."

All true statements—as far as they went.

Darin rubbed the back of his neck while he thought of what he wanted to say. "Right. And our father was the leader who brought the Kadir family to prominence after his father made the original deal with Kasht. Out of duty and loyalty to him and to the other elders, I feel my obligation is to gather as much information as possible.

"The Taj Zabbar have sworn to get even with us." Darin kept talking, wanting to impress hard truth on his brother. "We must make intelligent—and safe—decisions. We must be prepared before we act."

Using the power of his voice to make Shakir understand, Darin swallowed when his words sounded as rusty as an old scuttled ship. "You and Tarik have sacrificed for the family's sake. Just look at what you've done to date. You've put a hold on the security firm you and your buddies were trying to get off the ground. And Tarik. Tarik has resigned his commission from the U.S. Army."

Shakir shrugged, not looking directly at him but shifting his gaze to the windows. "We were both in good positions to lend our specialized knowledge to the family's efforts. You…" He let his words die as he waved a hand in Darin's direction.

"I am an expert in gaining information," Darin reiterated. "It's what I do for Kadir Shipping. I'm the one who investigates other firms for financial stability prior to takeover. I search through both public and private documents for authenticity. It's only fair that I share my expertise with the family as have my brothers."

Shakir threw up his hands. "Information retrieval is not fieldwork. Don't you see? You can help us the most by remaining at headquarters and leading the efforts at planning."

Darin knew Shakir was only worried for his safety, but he was done arguing. "Enough. I want to be reasonable, but my mind is made up. I'm the best person for this job and as the older brother, I am finished discussing it. And I'm late."

Darin pulled the conservative gray suit coat on over

his long-sleeved blue shirt and shot the cuffs. "Stick around if you want and back me up. But don't be too obvious about it."

He headed for the hotel-suite door but threw one last bit of sarcasm over his shoulder, the way he would have done during their teenage years. "Do you need me to remind you of covert protocols, little bro? If you do decide to stay and want to show up at the conference, play it smarter than most of your hoorah paratrooper buddies, will you? And…at the very least change your shirt."

Grinning to himself, Darin never turned around when he heard the crash of glass hitting the back of the door—at the exact moment as he'd stepped through and closed it. He picked up his pace and walked in haste to the elevator.

Rylie felt both tired and jet-lagged. The jet lag was new. The exhaustion was not.

She stepped off the public tram at a corner and took a few steps onto the wide boulevard known as Quai du Mont Blanc at the edge of Lake Geneva. Turning, she looked up the hill toward the city center twinkling at dusk with festive lights. Her old friend Marie Claire had given her directions for reaching the Presidents Hotel, where tonight's reception for the World Industry and Shipping conference was being held. But Marie Claire had also said it would be a lot easier to take a taxi. Rylie no longer had the cab fare to throw around.

Once again in her relatively short lifetime, Rylie Ann Hunt was reduced to taking public transportation. Coach airfare and buses. The sides of her mouth automatically turned up with the heartbroken memory as she thought about the delighted look on her mother's face the first time they'd taken a New York City shopping trip together after her daddy had hit it big. Rylie had suggested a cab.

"The Hunts no longer travel second-class, Rylie Ann," her mother said with a giddy laugh as she'd dragged her daughter into a limo. "It's first-class or nothing for these Texas gals from now on."

Remembering her mother in happier times, a more current picture formed in Rylie's mind. She knew exactly where her mama was today. Back in Midland in her tiny rental condo, sitting in an old borrowed rocker behind closed curtains, afraid to venture outside. Not a single smile had graced her mother's lips for six inconsolable months.

Rylie could not imagine what would've happened to her mother during the long days while Rylie was in the hospital, floating in and out of a drug-induced haze, if not for a few of her dad's old friends. And those friends would not let circumstances dissuade them, either, as they continued their care right up until today despite her mother's objections. There'd been a time when it was her mother who cared for others. But that same woman had aged twenty years practically overnight since the day of the explosion. She'd become a recluse. A broken spirit.

A chilly wind blew across the lake and hit Riley on the back of her neck. When that life-changing day of six months ago sneaked back into her mind, guilt lifted its nasty hand and smacked Rylie right across the face.

Even while good friends tried to make a difference, her mother had lost her lovely home and preferred to be isolated and alone rather than face the whispers and the possibility of bankruptcy. Riley, too, felt she was all alone no matter where she was. Alone to think. Alone to grieve…and to deal with her sorrow.

Daddy was dead. Riley still couldn't quite come to grips with the idea. But not one day went by that she didn't relive the explosion—and both her self-reproach and her anger grew.

Wrapping her arms around her middle and ignoring the ringing in her ears that occasionally returned when she was tired, Rylie trudged up the city street away from the lake, still going over in her mind what she could've done differently. The police and the insurance companies had said the explosion was an unfortunate accident caused by someone's carelessness at Hunt Drilling. She knew that wasn't true. So far the insurance investigators hadn't been able to prove their claims, either. Not one dime had been either paid out or denied yet.

Whether their company's fault or not, Rylie and her mother refused their lawyers' advice to wait until they were sued. In an effort to take care of the families of victims affected by the explosion who didn't have the benefit of insurance proceeds, Rylie and her mother chose to sell off everything they had and to liquidate much of their company to pay for things like funerals and hospital bills. Yet many debts still remained. Worse, through all of it, all the selling of her family's beloved things and all the pain of her burns and burst eardrums, Rylie's guilt about living when many others hadn't refused to die inside her and only gained power with each passing day.

The Kadir family must be responsible for the explosion and all this pain. It had to be them. Who else?

Perhaps their motive was insurance money. For whatever reason, they'd reduced her to nothing more than a lump of regret. The only thing keeping her going, keeping her plodding up this hill, was the need to prove them responsible for the explosion.

She would, too. Rylie was no less determined than a police dog on the scent and would find a way to prove the Kadirs were somehow connected. She couldn't find any other reason why a brand-new storage facility that had recently been safety checked and rechecked would suddenly explode.

In her quest for truth, Rylie had done her homework. Kadir Shipping always sent a representative to the World Industry and Shipping conference in Geneva. If the shipping business was anything like the drilling business, and she knew it would be, gossip was easy to come by at the conferences. After a day of long, boring speeches, attendees of these things normally let their hair down and drank too much at the evening get-togethers before having to confront another gruelling day.

A few questions. A couple of come-hither looks. Riley was ready to do anything to get what she wanted. What she must have. Proof. For this first party tonight, she could accept getting her hands on only a rumor—*if* that rumor would take her to the next step toward obtaining enough proof to accuse the Kadirs in public.

She'd been trying to swallow down her anger, but it was slowly taking over her soul as the months went by. She wouldn't readily admit it, but deep down she knew. The carefree young girl she had once been—the one who used to love everyone and needed everyone to love her in return—had changed forever. Her heart was quickly filling with hatred and her mind turning inward toward revenge. If she had looked in a mirror right then, Rylie wouldn't even have recognized herself through the grief and rage.

"Certainly, mademoiselle," the Frenchman politely told Rylie an hour later. "I am familiar with all Kadir Shipping representatives. A member of the Kadir family has been coming to our conferences for many years."

The middle-aged man in the navy wool suit smelling of mothballs turned in a half circle. "Yes, yes, I see Darin Kadir now."

He gestured to a small group of men nearby. "There, with several other gentlemen who also attend every year."

"Um, which one is he?"

Staring at her as if she were a bug who'd crawled up on the food table, the Frenchman gave her the once-over. Rylie knew she must look like she'd been sent through the spin cycle. Her singed hair, cut short after the explosion, had grown back in crazy curls, far beyond anyone's help. Her black dress was on loan from Marie Claire and too big. And her shoes were discount-store specials she'd bought right before leaving Texas.

Once upon a time, at her five-nine height, men had given her the once-over with a question mark, their gawking gradually evolving into lusty leers. But now that she had lost so much weight, she'd seen those same looks contorting into indifference or pity. And sure enough, the expression on the conference concierge's face when his glance landed on her loose dress and then popped back to her eyes turned to anxious concern.

"Are you all right, mademoiselle?"

She swiveled to study the group of men standing nearby. A Kadir family member was actually close enough to touch. At last she would start getting answers. But with her eagerness also came light-headedness as the colors in the room began bleeding together. Conversations ran down the walls like water.

Suddenly unsteady on her feet, Rylie nevertheless straightened her shoulders. "Yes, I'm fine. Just a little jet-lagged. Now which one was Mr. Kadir?"

After he pointed out a rather distinguished-looking younger man in a well-tailored suit, the concierge excused himself and wandered off. Rylie tried thinking of a way to wangle an introduction.

She leaned against the hors d'oeuvre table, reaching for calm and at the same time studying her enemy. The ringing in her ears began again in earnest. Starting at midlevel with the man's dark gray suit, she let her gaze roam up Darin Kadir's body to take in the wide shoulders. He must be well over six foot two. A good four or five inches taller than she was. She noted the expensive maroon tie knotted perfectly at his throat and above it the hard, square-cut jaw. The skin on his face, hands and throat had a golden glow that to her seemed far too dashing in the dim cocktail-party lights. His hair was that shiny raven color she'd never before believed could be for real. But on him...well, it was all too real.

He flicked a glance in her direction. She caught sight of midnight-black eyes, scrutinizing the party with keen intellect and a sensual but cold sort of perusal that many women would die for. He looked like a raptor about to pounce on prey. Rylie's knees wobbled as she put her hand out to grab on to the table like a lifeline.

Darin Kadir had the uncomfortable feeling that someone was watching him as his business associates began leaving his side, searching for the drink table. *Was someone from the Taj Zabbar family close by?* He absently touched the gun hidden under the suit coat at his back before glancing around the room once again.

He'd already learned the Taj Zabbar had sent family and business representatives to the conference this year. But so far, he had not run into any of them.

Catching sight of a tall woman standing at the food table watching him, he tried to decide if she was someone he had met before. She was obviously not part of the Taj Zabbar. Not with that curly dark red hair and fair complexion. But she did look vaguely familiar.

At that moment the woman's eyes closed and her legs appeared to give out. She went limp, slowly slipping toward the floor. He was at her side in an instant. Before he knew it, his arms were around her waist. He'd grabbed her intimately without as much as asking her permission.

She mumbled something he couldn't understand.

"Are you unwell? Can you stand on your own?"

She felt too insubstantial in his arms. All bones and skin and only a few bumps and curves in the right places to prove she was a woman. Not liking this forced involvement with a complete stranger, he nevertheless held on, hoping she would soon take charge of her own body.

"I…I guess I need to sit down." Her voice was as weak as a day-old tea bag.

Darin half carried and half dragged her to a quiet corner where a small overstuffed sofa sat vacant. He would rather the dwindling crowds at tonight's reception did not see this situation unfolding. He wanted no rumours. No questions. He'd been trying to blend in. In his opinion, rescuing a woman who was probably drunk would not be the best way of staying in covert mode and gaining information about the Taj Zabbar.

He tried to drop the deadweight of her body to the soft cushions, hoping to leave her in a comfortable position while he went to seek out the concierge. Someone else should take charge of her situation. But before he could let go and step back, she threw her arms around his neck and dragged him down beside her.

She clung to his arm like seaweed on the rocks during a squall. "You're Darin Kadir?"

Blinking at him frantically and then pinching her lips, she gazed over at him with singularly bright blue eyes. The color of the Mediterranean on a cloudless day, they bore into his with an expression that at once seemed dazed, confused and questioning. But as he looked again, he noted another, more shadowed emotion in those oceans that he could only guess at as rage— seething and deep. And directed at him?

Darin flinched and snapped his arm away from her biting fingers. Gazing into her face, he expected to have a hint of recognition. If she knew him, he must know her, too. He didn't. But what he did recognize was an unexpected kick of lust. Fascinated, he noticed she was beautiful, even considering the sharp angles of her too-thin cheeks.

"Yes. I'm Darin Kadir. Do I know you?"

"No." She spoke with more strength than he would've thought her capable of. "But you should. I'm your partner."

"Partner?" He sifted through his memory, trying to

come up with his connection to this stunning but strange woman. "Sorry, you need to fill me in. What's your name?"

"The name is Hunt, Kadir. Rylie Ann Hunt. I'm the new president of Hunt Drilling." Her eyes pinned him with a look that could've burned through stainless steel—incongruously making him think of superhuman strength.

As her name was beginning to register, she spat out a much stronger sentiment, sending a swift punch of regret directly to his gut. "At least what's left of it after you tried to blow us all straight to hell."

Chapter 2

Horrified by her own lack of self-control, Rylie pressed trembling fingertips to her lips, wishing she could take back the words. Why had she said that? She'd meant to be cool and conceal her true feelings. At least until she could coerce information from this man.

The festering bitterness boiling inside her was suddenly out there for the entire world to see. Her infamous impatience left her wide open. Would she never learn?

Darin leaned away from her, and his expression changed from what had appeared to be mild interest to a pucker of pure displeasure. "Miss Hunt, have you had too much to drink?"

Only a minute ago her overactive mouth was spouting off too much, and now she couldn't seem to get a word out. She shook her head fiercely and swallowed several times.

"No? Then I suggest you choose your words with more care." He stood, towering over her.

If looks could kill as easily as a chemical explosion, she would already be dead and in her grave.

"I am sorry for your loss," he said, dragging his sentence out on a harsh hiss. "But why would you say…"

Letting the words die in his mouth, he quickly glanced around the room and then tilted his head toward her. "Red Hunt was a well-respected oilman. He will be missed by the industry and his business associates. But as you must be aware, Kadir Shipping has already sent a team of attorneys to America to sort out the many claims, *and* to review our respective companies' currently complicated business association."

Rubbing a hand over his mouth, he looked as though he were choosing his words carefully. "In the meantime, I would recommend you refrain from making any statements to either a Kadir representative or to anyone else—especially in public—that you may regret in the future."

Struggling with both the light-headedness and the almost overpowering need to choke a confession out of this asshole, she screwed up her nerve and got to her feet. In league with terrorists or not, she needed Darin Kadir. Without him, Rylie knew she would never dig out the truth.

But once on her feet, her body swayed and she was forced to reach out and take his arm or else fall flat on her face. "Wait…"

His other hand closed around her biceps, keeping her from an embarrassing tumble but pulling her close against his chest instead. When she gazed into his eyes, her emotions began a roller-coaster ride. Deep within those coal-black irises she caught sight of a flash of—need.

Need? Hell's bells. In the eyes of an arrogant terrorist? Or perhaps she'd been all wrong, and he was only a businessman who had no scruples and was trying to scam the insurance companies for big bucks. Either way, *need* was the last thing she'd expected to see in his eyes.

Taking a step back and planting her feet, she held his gaze, searching for any reason why she should find herself in such sudden turmoil over a man she had vowed to unmask as a murderer. In the next instant, she could swear she sensed loneliness in him—and a glint of something else. Something much deeper she couldn't put a name to, coming from the same hidden recesses of his steady stare.

Then the moment was gone and his blank eyes were devoid of any expression save for irritation. But Rylie was shaken by what she'd seen.

As usual during times of stress, babbling words began spewing from her too-loud mouth. "I think I must be jet-lagged. I didn't mean... I apologize, Mr. Kadir... uh...Darin."

He let go of her arm and a wary look crept into his eyes. Not good. She didn't want him to be on guard. Now she would have to start all over again and figure out ways to make him trust her.

Her knees wobbled once more, and she decided any information-gathering efforts would have to wait for another day. "I could stand some sleep, but I would like to talk to you when I can make more sense. How about tomorrow? Can we set up a time to get together?" Teetering on her narrow heels, she hung on to his arm.

He shook his head slowly and she knew he was about to turn her down. "I have a heavy conference agenda all day tomorrow." Taking her by the shoulders, he eased her backward and helped her sit down on the couch. "But perhaps we could find a few free minutes after the workshops and before the evening banquet. Shall I plan to come to your hotel around five?"

Well, what do you know? Amazed by his sudden change of heart, she was too thrilled to ask why and take the chance of messing things up.

"Uh, no, not to my place." She wasn't registered at a hotel but didn't want him to know she was staying on Marie Claire's couch. "How about we meet at your hotel? Where are you staying?"

Tight lines formed around his eyes. "Let's compromise. There's a club…pub…bar, I guess Americans would say, called Arthur's Rive Gauche. It's rather more elegant than I would normally choose for conversation and it's wildly popular, but I'm sure we can find a quiet corner. Why don't I meet you there at half past five?"

"That'll be fine. Great." She made a move to rise, wanting to show him she could be perfectly civilized by shaking his hand. But she hadn't even made it to her feet before the dizziness returned and threw her back into the cushions.

"Stay seated," he insisted. "I'll search out the concierge and have him bring you a plate of food. Eating may give you a much-needed temporary energy boost. However, I have no hope of it stilling your temper or mouth." He cocked his head and waited for her to make a comment.

When she didn't, he added, "A little sustenance might at least provide you with enough strength to take a cab back to your hotel. Allow me to arrange it, Miss Hunt?"

She closed her eyes and leaned back—for only a moment. "All right, but please call me Rylie. And thanks."

"You must be joking, brother." Shakir lounged in one of the club chairs of their hotel suite several hours later, with a bottle of dark ale in his hand and a smirk across his face. "Rylie Hunt had the nerve to accost you and bloody well accuse you of murder?"

"You should've seen the look in her eyes," Darin told him. "It was enough to raise the hairs on the back of even your tough paratrooper's leather neck."

Shakir sat up straighter. "You don't think she could be some kind of spy or lookout for the Taj Zabbar family, do you? It would make a kind of perverse sense. I know if I was into subterfuge and covert warfare, using a woman who has reason to hate the world would be perfect. Who knows what lies they could've told her in an effort to make her bend to their will."

Darin gave it a moment's consideration and quickly discarded the idea. "Not this woman. I have the feeling she could spot a liar from a mile away, and I doubt anyone on earth could bend her to their will. But I've agreed to meet with her. I need to uncover what she already knows."

"Bad move." Shakir screwed up his mouth. "You can't seriously mean to get close to this woman. She could be dangerous. Why would you agree to do such a thing?"

"I felt sorry for her." But that wasn't strictly the truth.

He'd felt something, all right. But the something was pure, unrefined and nearly uncontrollable…lust.

Theoretically, his sudden all-consuming erotic need should've been tempered by his empathy for her situation. After all, his life had been altered irrevocably with that explosion the same as hers. But the trouble with theories was they weren't real life. In reality, despite what he should have felt, he'd searched his memory and couldn't come up with a time when a stranger, or anyone at all, had affected him with quite this much seething passion.

He wasn't sure why, either. She was a little too tall, a little too thin and a little too loud for his taste. Her overall appearance reminded him of what he'd always considered the looks of a spoiled girl from America's western lands. Over-the-top—in every way. Not in the least his normal type of companion when it came to the opposite sex.

His brother was still seated, staring absently at the half-empty beer bottle in his hand. "This is not a good idea." Shakir shook his head forcefully. "Even if she isn't working with the Taj Zabbar, let's suppose one of them spots the two of you together. That might give rise to a lot of false assumptions. False assumptions that could be life-threatening—to her or to you."

"Don't worry," Darin told him, letting his voice carry a cavalier tone he was certainly not feeling. "I've suggested our meeting take place in a pub that's popular with the locals but is out of the way for conference attendees. No one will spot us there."

Later that same night in the dimly lit lobby bar of Darin's hotel, Sheik Newaf Bin Hamad Taj Zabbar hung up his satellite phone when he spotted his distant cousin Samman Taweel walking his way. The young, hollow-eyed fellow weaved past several empty tables heading straight for him.

"Sit." Sheik Hamad gestured to the chair across from him with the glowing tip of his Cuban Cohiba Behike. "I assume you left a compatriot to watch Darin Kadir. Is this so?"

"Yes, my sheik. The target you asked me to watch has seemingly retired to his room for the evening. One of the other men you hired is watching his door."

"Very well. Then tell me what you observed of our target's behavior at the conference reception."

This distant cousin was far from brilliant. But Hamad had not hesitated to employ the dull but desperate man, because desperate men follow instructions exactly. Since the Taj Zabbar clan was finally on the cusp of exacting their ultimate revenge for the subjugation and humiliation they'd endured for centuries, he needed men like this one. Hamad knew better than to take a chance on hiring outsiders when his clan was close to their goals. The money was flowing. Let the retribution begin.

But patience was the key. For now, his goal was to detect new ways of embarrassing and humiliating three of the most important young Kadir men, the sons of the most powerful Kadir elder. Three of the Taj Zabbar's greatest enemies.

Hamad wasn't worried. Like this cousin, those rising Kadir stars didn't seem like any great geniuses. And Hamad would accept nothing less than full capitulation from them in the end. He had little doubt his clan's retribution would come to pass exactly as he'd planned.

The entire Kadir clan would soon suffer in the same ways as the Taj Zabbar had suffered throughout hundreds of miserable years. He was counting on it.

Cousin Taweel's hoarse yet respectful voice broke into his thoughts. "At the reception the target approached a pretty young woman and the two sat down together. They spoke for several minutes and then, before abandoning her, our target arranged with a concierge to see to the woman's comfort. Food and taxi service back to her hotel."

Hamad thought such behavior unexpected for the disciplined and rigid eldest Kadir son, and all exceptions from the ordinary worried him. "Did Kadir and this woman seem to be close friends? Did you find out who she was?"

"They appeared to be on most intimate terms, my sheik." As he spoke, a tic appeared near an eyebrow, telling Hamad of his conservative cousin's obvious disapproval.

Hamad didn't consider either the disapproval or Kadir's behavior important.

"I was told the name of the woman is Hunt. From America."

Hunt. What would one of the Hunts be doing at a shipping conference? Hamad did not care for the idea. Had Darin Kadir invited the woman here to share information?

The Taj Zabbar elders had decided on temporary surveillance of the Kadir brothers rather than an outright attack. Extreme secrecy was essential for their revenge to succeed. Plans still had to be finalized and everything had to remain undercover until it was too late for their enemies to stop the schemes. But if it were true that

Darin Kadir already suspected the Texas explosion was not an accident, his life would shortly come crashing to an abrupt end. It was Hamad's duty to make it so.

Leaning back, Hamad tried easing his tension by chewing on the cigar. He felt positive that each detail in Texas had been dealt with cleverly, that nothing had been left to chance. The shipping facility explosion had been judged an accident, exactly the way Hamad planned it. Of course, he had anticipated the blame for the *accident* to accrue to Kadir Shipping instead of to Hunt Drilling the way their foolish American law enforcement believed. But the results were nearly the same. Kadir business interests had taken a loss, both financially and in reputation. All in all, it had been an excellent first shot in the Taj Zabbar's war of retribution.

Hunt Drilling was only unfortunate collateral damage, as the Americans would say. His sources told him the Hunt organization had been fatally weakened and that the remaining Hunt family felt extraordinary anger toward the Kadirs. Had that changed?

Hamad needed to understand this new development. His plans could well depend on finding out what the Hunt woman knew—or thought she knew.

The flame had gone out of his cigar and he used the tip to make his point to the cousin. "I want to talk to this Hunt woman. Is it possible to find out where she is staying? Can you question her taxi driver?"

The young Taweel lowered his eyelids and shook his head slowly.

Growing impatient, Hamad tapped his cigar against the tabletop. "I will put out a few requests. Perhaps we can locate her hotel yet tonight. In the meantime, you are to remain with Darin Kadir. When he leaves his rooms, do not let him out of your sight. If he meets with that woman again, I want to be notified. And then, bring her to me."

"You may be requesting an impossible task, my sheik. What if the woman does not wish to come?"

The cigar tip tapped rapidly against the table as Hamad held frustration in check. "Then you must insist. Or…" Tap. Tap. Tap. "Just see that you bring her to me."

It was nearing 2:00 a.m. when Hamad Taj Zabbar placed his last phone call of the night. Frustration had decimated his posture since he had sent his cousin away an hour earlier. His shoulders were strung tight from the strain.

The Hunt woman was not registered in any hotel in the city. Due to the late hour, Hamad had been forced to give up his search. It was possible she'd registered at any number of inns, bed-and-breakfasts or hostels, and he would never be able to hunt through every one.

Unaccustomed to not winning each skirmish he entered, Hamad rubbed his temple, vowing that his failure to locate the Hunt woman right away would be only a minor setback.

Hamad felt confident that even his dull cousin could bring her to him at the first opportunity.

Taweel had better.

The next morning Darin rolled his feet out of bed and hung his head in his hands. What a long night it had been.

Dreams of drowning in vibrant blue-green eyes had kept him tossing for hours on end. He'd been lost in luxurious layers of auburn curls. Soft and shiny, so smooth against his skin. Like a bath in velvet.

What a fool he was. The urge to pound his fists into his empty head drove him to stand. Perhaps a shower would help. As he walked to the bath, it became clear he had better dredge up some of his infamous impassivity. It should come easy for him, as he'd been accused of being aloof and detached for most of his life.

Right now he could use some of that lethal remoteness. He'd not needed anyone, save for his two brothers, since his mother's death. Women were friends, business associates and overnight flings, and this was no time for his libido to begin overruling his head. The middle of his first covert operation for the family would be the worst time to undertake a romantic relationship with a woman he barely knew.

While cranking the cold water on high, Darin thought of a brilliant plan. As soon as he stepped from the shower, he would find out as much as he could about Rylie Hunt's background. No one could withstand his kind of scrutiny. No one. He was positive that the more he learned about Rylie the more this crazy obsession of his would wane.

Yes, a good plan. Such a good plan that he began to whistle. Until…he stepped into the shower and a shot of freezing water hit him flat in the chest.

As he swore, the first image that came into his mind was Rylie's. Completely naked and lingering under the shower with him. Hell. Perhaps no plan would be good enough to rid him of his passion.

"Rylie, you asked me to wake you while it was still early. I've made a pot of tea."

Marie Claire's lilting voice caused Rylie to lift

her scratchy eyelids and rouse herself from a fitful morning's dream. She managed to sit up and put her feet on the rose-patterned carpet, but her T-shirt was wet with sweat. Her bones were still stiff from tossing and turning. Her mind still reeling from another night of seeing fire and smoke in her dreams.

Yawning, she glanced toward the rain oozing down a windowpane. Unlike Texas gully-washers, the wetness here seemed damp and depressing without being cleansing. Only enough mist and fog to frizz the hair and muddy the boots.

"Did you get enough rest?" Marie Claire sat in the one other chair in the room and began pouring them both cups of fragrant tea. "I'm not sure my sofa is comfortable. No one has ever stayed the night on it before and it's too short for someone of your height."

"The sofa was fine." Rylie lied to her old college roommate as she reached for her tea cup. "I appreciate your hospitality. I'm not sure what I would've done if you hadn't invited me to stay."

Marie Claire gave her an I-know-you-and-you-would've-found-a-way look before blowing on her own steaming cup and glancing at Rylie over the rim. "I was searching the Internet for info on the Kadir family this morning. You seem convinced that they're the bad guys and I can't quite figure out why. I wanted to know more about them."

Rylie felt the muscles in her face soften. Her dear friend had given up free time to help with Rylie's important mission.

"I could've told you most of their background information if you'd asked. Between the original lawyers for our business merger and my own private investigators,

I'm sure I know everything worth knowing about the Kadirs."

Sitting back in her chair, Marie Claire's lips pursed, making her look like a pixie with a secret. "Oh really? Then will you tell me more about the Kadir–Taj Zabbar family feud? Start all the way back in the fifteen hundreds, okay?"

A sudden swallow of hot tea burned Rylie's tongue and left her sputtering. "What feud? And who are the Taj Zabbar?"

"The reason I was asking is because I couldn't find an explanation for the feud online." Marie Claire shrugged a freckled shoulder. "Just a mention of the Taj Zabbar holding their grudge for a long time. I do know a little about the Taj Zabbar clan, though. They live in a desolate place in the Middle East called Zabbaran. For centuries their territory was ruled by neighboring countries. One neighbor, Kasht, took over their land about a hundred years ago. The Taj Zabbar mounted a couple of rebellions along the way, but they never could break free.

"Then about two years ago, the Taj Zabbar managed to liberate themselves from Kasht, shaking off their oppressors with help from the world community." Marie Claire took a sip of tea before raising her eyebrows. "Now it seems the Taj Zabbar family is suddenly rich. An ocean of oil has been discovered under their land."

Dang. Marie Claire had sprung this new twist on her without warning. Rylie took pride in her information-gathering ability and had thought she'd been prepared.

Well…looked like maybe not so much. She'd apparently missed something important. An ancient feud and gushers of money made it sound as if the Kadir–Taj Zabbar situation could be potentially dangerous to not only Hunt Drilling but the rest of the world.

Still Rylie couldn't put all the pieces together. She was still missing something. Why? What was behind the feud, and could it have something to do with an explosion as far away as Texas?

Chapter 3

Looking over the busy club at masses of people, Darin caught a glimpse of wild auburn hair in a far corner. Meeting Rylie here had sounded like a good idea yesterday. But now that it was happy hour and the place was packed with young professionals, he wasn't so sure.

He made his way through the boisterous bodies, still wondering if tonight's meeting was smart. It was possible his brother had been right last night. Despite his erotic dreams of her, Rylie Hunt could be in the employ of the Taj Zabbar, and talking to her might be dangerous. After all, he was a businessman. What did he really know about covert operations?

He knew one thing for sure: Rylie was who she said she was. He'd found pictures on the Internet of Red Hunt's daughter in accounts of the explosion. But was she also a gorgeous and deadly spy? He couldn't know that for certain unless he talked to her.

He'd asked around about her this morning and checked with others back at his office. He now knew that she'd spent weeks in the hospital after the explosion. Since her release, she'd also taken a few altruistic business steps above and beyond what Darin considered reasonable.

Admirable? Perhaps. Foolhardy? Very likely.

Did that necessarily mean she was not also involved with the Taj Zabbar? He had to coerce her into opening up to him in order to find out.

Her table was located in an alcove and seemed relatively quiet. As he arrived, she glanced over at him and froze. Even in the inadequate lighting, he noted that her pupils were dilated and her expression frazzled. Her face was a deathly shade of gray that seemed more pronounced in proximity to her black denim jacket and jeans. Her lips tensed and she crossed her arms tightly against her chest. Shrunken in on herself, she looked like a housefly suddenly caught up in a sticky web and docilely expecting the spider.

His heart thumped once and went out to her. If she was as innocent as she appeared, Rylie Hunt had no reason to fear a Kadir.

He simply could not put the picture she made sitting there, her whole body trembling, together in his mind with a Taj Zabbar spy.

When he got closer, two bloodred spots appeared on her cheeks and tears backed up in her eyes. For a moment Darin's only thoughts were of calming her by taking her in his arms. Instead, he slid into the lone empty chair at her table with his back to the corner.

But it was all he could do not to reach out and cover her quivering hands with his own.

"Hello," she said in a shaky voice. "I wondered if you would really show up."

"I'm here." He nodded at the waiter to get his attention and ordered himself a sparkling water and Rylie a glass of pinot grigio, hoping the lighter drink would calm her nerves without sending her into some alcoholic stupor.

After the waiter acknowledged the order and left, all was quiet at their table and Darin took a moment to look around the club. Rylie had put them in the best possible spot for quiet conversation. No one around them was paying any attention.

A couple of young lovebirds at the closest table, who might have been near enough to hear what was being said, were kissing and whispering with their foreheads touching together and their hands touching everywhere else. Impervious to all around them. Darin was almost jealous of the way they blocked out the world. His relationships were never so intense.

Bringing himself back to his immediate surroundings, Darin felt confident enough that he and Rylie were isolated in the middle of a crowd. They could talk freely.

"Why?" Her voice was a bit stronger, a bit lower than yesterday.

Shaking his head at the out-of-place question, he was beginning to wonder if that explosion had affected her mind.

"Why are you here?" she blurted before he could say anything. "I wouldn't think a Kadir would be willing to talk to a Hunt."

Surprised by the question, but interested in where she was going with this line, he chuckled and gave her a polite nod. "Now it's my turn to ask—why not? You don't have plans to do me harm, do you?"

She didn't answer, but before the lull in the conversation dragged into an embarrassing void, her wine and his water arrived. Her lack of a response, to both his question and his companionable attitude, did nothing to fill him with confidence. He had expected either a lie or an accusation. She confused him with a simple blank stare.

Rylie took a sip of wine and kept on staring at him. He felt as though he were a rat being studied in a scientific experiment, and he wasn't crazy about the idea. Being too closely scrutinized had to be bad for covert operations. The longer she stared, the more he wondered if she was, in fact, working for the Taj Zabbar.

A spark appeared in her eyes. But before Darin could figure out if that spark meant a change of mood or something more dangerous, she asked, "Would you mind telling me about the Kadir and Taj Zabbar feud?"

In the middle of lifting his water to his lips, Darin choked, spilling the drink down the front of his button-down shirt.

"What did you say?" he sputtered. "Who told you anything about the Taj Zabbar?"

Leaning in toward him, she hurriedly dabbed at his chest with a paper napkin. Tiny smile lines appeared at the corners of her eyes. It was the first easy expression he'd seen on her face and the casualness of it made her glow. How beautiful would she be if she ever actually laughed?

He couldn't imagine, but the mere idea made him want to see for himself.

Before Darin could give her an automatic grin, he ordered up the covert operative inside him and brushed her hands away. "Forget the shirt. The water will dry. Tell me what you know about the Taj Zabbar."

"All I know is what a friend read on the Internet." She sat back in her chair and looked as though she was poised to run. "The Taj Zabbar is in control of their own country again after nearly five hundred years of being oppressed by neighbors. And they apparently hate the Kadir family for some reason, but I can't find out why."

When he said nothing, she continued, "I do know the Kadirs weren't the ones who enslaved them. You folks don't even have your own country, do you? Why would they carry a grudge against your family?"

Under her shower of questions, Darin felt his jaw and shoulders tightening. He tried to relax. Beyond the obvious lust, what was it about her that so intrigued him?

If this was some kind of game, he would play along until he was satisfied she wasn't working for the enemy.

"I suppose I can tell you the family legends of the Taj Zabbar feud. But then I have a question or two for you. Do you promise to answer truthfully?"

"Why should I?"

"Because otherwise this conversation is over. I have business matters that need attention."

Her lip jutted out and her eyes narrowed. "Okay. Maybe. But I reserve the right not to answer."

She frustrated him beyond belief. "We'll see about

that." He tried to find some emotion he could pin down in her eyes, but all he found was hunger.

"Wait a second." He lifted a hand, palm out. "I've decided there is one more condition. I'm going to order something for you to eat and I want you to eat every bite—or else no more conversation."

Her mouth gaped open. "What is with you and the compulsion to feed me?"

"It's just your tough luck that you picked this Kadir to harass. I won't be responsible for you collapsing from hunger while you're with me. And you look like you could be blown over by a light breeze. Is it a deal?"

"Fine," she muttered. "Do you think this place serves salads?" She rolled her eyes. "Don't I look like I need to diet?"

Nearly done chowing down on the huge bowl of pasta and seafood Darin had insisted she order, Rylie was trying to calm her racing mind. For the last thirty minutes, Darin had been almost overly polite. Talking casually about the chill in the air or the newly budded spring blossoms on the trees seemed bizarre. The evening was starting to feel like a date, except that his eyes kept darting around the room as if he were expecting someone else to show up.

Somehow over the last twenty-four hours, Rylie's anger toward the Kadirs—or at least toward this Kadir—seemed to have subsided. She tried to dredge up a chunk of that old hatred, but all she came up with was curiosity.

She dropped her fork and blotted her mouth with a napkin. "Done. Will you—please—tell me the story of the feud now?"

"It isn't a true feud. Feuds take two parties. The Kadirs have not held a grudge against the Taj Zabbar—in the past."

The way he added that last part was curious. She made a mental note to ask about it later. But in the meantime, Darin sat back in his chair and sipped his sparkling water as if he was done talking. Like hell.

When she glared at him and fisted her hands on the table, he lifted the corners of his mouth and rolled his eyes. "All right. I guess I did promise. There's an old legend about the family's first encounter with the Taj Zabbar—over five centuries ago. Is that what you want?"

"To start."

"Yes, well… For nearly a thousand years the Kadir clan have been nomads and traders. Originally we traveled the Spice Route in ten-mile-long caravans, staying for a time with the various peoples we met along the way. Our clan never claimed any lands as our own but would rely on the kindness of those who would allow us to pitch our tents on their land."

Rylie leaned back in her chair and listened to him speak in that dreamy voice of his. As he spoke, she thought about the Arabian Nights tales. His hushed words tied her in a web of romance, destiny and mystic promise. Visions of sandstorms and camels and dark sheiks riding across dunes on horseback swam in her mind.

"At around sixteen hundred AD," he went on, "the Kadir caravan arrived in a new territory. A land of vast, isolated deserts and rough mountain terrain. A land with easily accessible coastlines for commerce. The Kadirs found the territory was inhabited by a fierce warrior tribe called the Taj Zabbar."

Darin was finally getting down to the legend. "The Kadirs have always come and gone in peace, no matter where they've traveled." Shooting a quick glance around at the thinning crowds in the bar, he continued. "But the Taj Zabbar wanted no trade and no peace. Our people were preparing to move on when the caravan was attacked. Taj Zabbar warriors robbed, raped and murdered many of our people before the Kadirs could mount a defense."

He'd stopped talking and a faraway look appeared in his eyes. Rylie wondered if the magic of the legend was affecting him the same way it did her.

"Don't stop now. What happened next?"

"What? Oh, sorry." He suddenly looked annoyed and Rylie was about to ask why when he said, "Do you see anyone watching us?"

She pivoted in her chair and checked around the bar. "Nope. Why?"

His lips narrowed into a grimace. "Nothing. It's just…

"Never mind. Where was I?"

"Your ancestors defending themselves against attack."

She couldn't quite name the expression in his eyes, but in a moment he began his story once more.

"The Kadirs successfully defended themselves. But by then the caravan was destroyed. It would've been impossible for them to move on in the shape they were in. They were compelled to settle down where they were for long enough to repopulate their herds of camels and horses and to construct new tents. A second generation of our people had been born before the caravan was ready to travel again."

"Wow. So, like, years, then? What about the Taj Zabbar during that time?"

"Yes, it was many years. And the Taj Zabbar continued their raids on our people." Darin's voice dropped to a near whisper and she was forced to lean forward to hear what he was saying. "Finally, in desperation, the Kadir elders decided they had no choice but to fight back. They rounded up as many of the Taj Zabbar as they could, executing the worst of the murderers and dispersing the rest."

Rylie felt a whiff of air on the back of her neck at that moment and looked around to see if someone had opened a door behind her. She found the bar crowds had thinned considerably, and the door was firmly shut against the night air. She could barely believe she'd been so entranced by the story that she hadn't even noticed the time.

Darin kept talking and she whipped her head back to hear what he was saying. "After the Kadir clan left their territory for good, the Taj Zabbar rulers and warriors had been so decimated that they couldn't defend themselves. Their neighbors swarmed over their lands and enslaved what was left of the tribe." Darin shook his head at his own words, which seemed a little strange to her.

"The Taj Zabbar never forgot or forgave the Kadirs, I suppose."

"No. Not for the following five hundred years."

"But it's over now, isn't it?" she demanded. "I mean, the Taj Zabbar finally got their territory back a couple of years ago. All the problems between your clans were long ago."

"Not exactly."

She thought about what he'd said at the start of his story.... *Our first encounter with the Taj Zabbar—*

"Something else has happened since? What?"

Darin raised his eyebrows. "Sorry. It's my turn to ask the questions."

"But…"

"Uh-uh." His face lit up like he'd been given a special present. "A promise is a promise."

He was right about that. She believed in honoring a promise, too.

But she didn't have to like it. "Fine," she grumbled. "What do want to know?"

Taking his time, Darin raised his glass and swallowed the last of his wine. "First, I would like an explanation of why you threw that accusation around last night about me causing the explosion?"

Struck, as if by his hand across her face, Rylie drew in a breath. "I didn't mean *you* exactly. I was talking about…"

"My family?" he suggested. "But even that doesn't make any sense. My uncle was killed in the explosion the same as your father. Thinking logically, why would the Kadirs kill a member of their family and cost their own company untold amounts of trouble and aggravation?"

"I…" It did sound ridiculous now hearing him say it. How would she explain herself?

The ugly truth was all she had to offer, but she vowed to take the punishing embarrassment that came with it like her father's daughter should. "I wasn't thinking clearly, I guess. Maybe I thought the explosion was some sort of suicide bombing."

"Terrorism? You thought we…" He stopped talking and the strangest look crossed his face.

His shoulders raised and straightened as he glared at her. "Certainly an educated person wouldn't let prejudice cloud their mind in such dark ways. You seem too sophisticated for racial profiling."

"I am." She heard the desperation in her voice and wondered why this man's opinion of her had suddenly become so important. "I mean, I don't really believe any of that stuff. But my judgment has been impaired since the explosion—since the death of my father. I…I haven't been completely well. Obviously."

It took him a second, but the hard expression in his eyes finally softened to sympathy as he said, "Which brings me to my next question. Why are you here? You should be home with your family and running what's left of your company."

She tightened her lips and glared at him, not ready to discuss this yet.

"I learned this morning that you have nearly bankrupted yourself and the entire Hunt firm," he continued. "All in an effort to lessen the suffering for victims of the explosion—every one of them, and not only Hunt employees. That may be admirable, but what good are you doing them or yourself by coming here?"

The question made her stop and think. Why was she here? What had she hoped to accomplish?

"Justice." Once she'd spoken the word aloud, it made sense. "I want to give the dead and injured justice. I am positive that explosion wasn't caused by any accident. It was deliberate. And I intend to find out who caused it and why."

* * *

Still stunned by a couple of things Rylie had said, Darin ignored the creepy sensation of being watched as he paid their bill and ushered her outside. He'd checked out every person remaining in the club before they left, but he couldn't pinpoint anyone who appeared to be spying on them.

He wasn't the kind of person who ordinarily gave himself over to fantasy. But he thought perhaps it was the strong sense of responsibility toward Rylie that he'd been experiencing that was making him paranoid on her behalf.

Her mention of justice had stopped him. He understood her sentiments and her loyalty to her father. Justice went along with honor and family loyalty. But on the other hand, for centuries the Taj Zabbar had used their quest for justice as an excuse for threats and dishonest behavior toward his family.

Justice was not a concept he took lightly. Over the last hour, he'd begun to reconsider some of the steps that the Kadirs had already taken against the Taj Zabbar— without any proof. Where was the justice in building a defensive line and spying operations without knowing for sure that the Taj Zabbar were already at war?

One thing would definitely be different for him after tonight. Darin felt confident Rylie was not involved with the Taj Zabbar in any way. She was merely a grieving victim, trying to make sense out of the nonsensical.

Death had a way of turning normally smart people into hysterical idiots. He knew that because he'd been there himself at least once. When his mother died, Darin had been ready to blame anyone and everyone—except the cancer that killed her.

Those thoughts made him wonder if the death of one of their own hadn't also sent the Kadir elders into that same spiral of frantic paranoia. Both he and Rylie might be better off to quit their respective witch hunts and go back to work.

Gently laying a hand at her waist to help guide her through the doorway and outside to the walkway, Darin thought back on the other stunning thing she'd said tonight. Or perhaps it wasn't what she'd said but the way she'd said it.

She had been wrapped up in the tale of his family when she'd looked up at him and demanded he finish the story. He'd gotten a good look at her eyes. Those eyes with their oceans of emotions had totally lost their anger. Instead, he spotted something else in them that he hadn't expected.

Destiny. Preordained and undeniable. One day soon, they were fated to be together. Whether for one night, one week or forever, he could not say. But he was as sure of her as he was of the rising sun in the morning.

"I think I can manage to make it back on my own," she said as her voice broke through his thoughts. "Thank you for the dinner and the history lesson."

Not a chance. He wasn't letting her go anywhere alone.

Before he could tell her that, a man appeared at the curb directly in front of her. A Middle Eastern man in the clan keffiyeh of the Taj Zabbar held his palms out as if pleading with her to understand. Rylie came to an abrupt halt and Darin could sense her tension in the way she held her body.

His own body was as tight as the skin on a conga drum. Sweat trickled at his temple. He prepared himself for defense, trying desperately to remember everything he had learned.

"Excuse me," the man muttered in hesitant English. "Miss Hunt, my employer wishes to speak with you. You will come now?"

"How do you know my name?"

The man gave a tentative glance over her shoulder toward Darin. "You will come now, please. My employer insists." He reached out and took her by the arm.

And for Darin, everything changed.

Chapter 4

Damn it. Just when she was starting to like Darin, it turned out he'd been lying. How stupid could she be?

Letting him lead her right into a trap.

Rylie ripped her arm out of the stranger's grasp and stomped down hard on the man's foot. As the guy yelled and danced around in pain, she rounded on Darin. But before she could rear back and jam her knee to his groin, Darin shot out of her reach. Next thing she knew, he was punching the strange man dressed in Middle Eastern garb and knocking him off his feet. With one smooth motion, Darin whirled and grabbed her around the waist, lifting her off her feet. He half dragged and half carried her down the mist-dampened sidewalk in the opposite direction of the man lying in the street.

"Move," he growled in her ear.

"I'm not going anywhere. Not with that guy and

not with you." Balling her fists, she tried smacking Darin's face.

Her efforts were ineffective because her feet were dangling in midair and she couldn't get adequate force behind her swings. Darin never missed a step on the slick, uneven cobblestones. She gave a good show of kicking him, but he was moving too fast and her toes were still barely touching the ground.

They made it around the next three city street corners using the same combined running and crablike moves before Darin finally slowed, turned and checked behind them. He never loosened his hold on her, not even a little.

"Let me go." She gulped in air while her heartbeat raced like a motorcycle engine.

"You were terrific back there," Darin whispered, breathing hard. "Quit fighting me. If you act stupid now, he'll catch up to us again. I think there's a small hotel in the next block. I'm sure we can make it that far, and we'll have the doorman summon a taxi and be long gone before your assailant ever comes to his senses."

She'd heard real respect for her actions in the tone of his voice and it helped to put a stopper in her fear. "Let me down," she said calmly. "I can run faster if you'll let me go."

Rylie had no intention of going anywhere with Darin, but together they would have a better shot at getting away. She could give him the slip later. Right this minute, he was the devil she knew.

Darin loosened his grip and lowered her to her feet. She was amazed he had actually believed what she'd said and her mouth dropped open. For a moment she stared into his trusting eyes. Then she turned and ran.

"Split up and double back," she hollered over her shoulder. "I'll meet you—"

She never had a chance to finish the thought because Darin caught her from behind, gripped her arm and kept up the momentum she'd begun as the two of them dashed down the half-lit sidewalks hand in hand. He might be trusting, but it seemed he wasn't stupid.

Out of breath, they made it to the doorstep of an inn. Banging on the locked door with one fist, Darin kept his other hand glued tightly to hers. Apparently he was also familiar with the concept behind the saying "Fool me once…"

A particularly grumpy innkeeper finally let them in after Darin explained their circumstances in the man's native French. Rylie wasn't sure, but the memory of her old college French led her to believe Darin had also mentioned a bonus for calling them a cab.

Within a few minutes, money had changed hands and she was safely tucked into the backseat of a beat-up Mercedes taxicab.

Suddenly exhausted, Rylie leaned her body against the strength of Darin's shoulder. "Where are we going? To the police?"

No answer.

A sneaky thought of betrayal crept into her mind. Could he be one of the bad guys after all?

"Okay," she said in a meek tone…at least it sounded meek considering that the tone came from her own loud mouth. "No police. Then at least tell me where we're headed. I kinda thought you and I were beginning a real friendship back at the bar. You owe me…"

"Friends don't lie to each other."

"When did I lie? You were the one who lied to me."

She forced this new white lie out with an indignant groan as if she'd meant it, but that was the best she could muster. Of course she'd lied in the middle of trying to escape. She wasn't a fool, and she would have done anything to get away. But if he pushed her too hard, she might crumble in a heap on the cab floor and beg for his forgiveness now that he'd saved her life.

"I do not lie." His tone was hurt instead of incensed, and she felt a very real pang of regret.

"Okay…" Suddenly needing to find a little backbone and a lot of pride, she steadied her voice. "Then who was that guy? And I want the truth."

"I have never seen the man before."

Screwing up her mouth for a few well-chosen words, she was about to let them loose when he continued, "But I did recognize him as Taj Zabbar. He wore the purple-checked head cloth of their modern-day businessmen."

"Businessman? Bull. That assailant, as you called him, was far more interested in kidnapping than business."

The next thought came out of her mouth much too easily. "Hey. Talking about kidnapping, he was after *me,* not you. What the heck would the Taj Zabbar want with me, anyway?"

Her words lingered in the stale air of the backseat as the cab jerked around corners and then over one of the Rhône River bridges. Interesting question, wasn't it? She could almost feel Darin mulling the same idea over in his head.

"If you're not lying again," he began in a sober tone, "then that's something we must learn together."

His voice was rigid, unyielding, but as he spoke he

gently folded her hand in his. He glanced over at her, and if she'd been talking, his expression would've surprised her speechless. Instead of a glare of suspicion, his eyes plainly said he thought she was the most exquisite and priceless creature he had ever beheld. A tiny shiver ran to the base of her spine at the sensual look in his eyes. This was not the gaze of a man who wanted only friendship and truth.

Rylie was unsure of what she wanted, so she left her hand right where it was. The idea of kissing him...and more...was certainly appealing. Being this close to a man as exotic and enticing as this one was driving fire through her veins.

Still, she didn't know him. Not really. And someone— maybe someone he knew well—was trying to kidnap her.

Darin spoke to the cabbie in French and the driver made a couple of quick left turns, heading for the expensive part of town. A few more minutes of riding in quiet and the cab pulled up in front of the Geneva Four Seasons Hotel, a spendy and trendy joint that was far above Rylie's current circumstances. She looked up at the bright lights and marbled entry and wondered how much this place could possibly cost per night—and then couldn't help thinking how many hospital bills she could've paid with all that money.

The cab stopped, Darin threw a wad of Swiss francs at the driver and then eased her out with a nod to the doorman holding the open cab door.

When Rylie put her none-too-steady feet on the pavement, Darin reached for her. He pulled her close and took a moment to study her under the light. She knew she must look a mess, all sweaty and disheveled.

Trying to break free, her only thought was getting away from both his intensity and the harsh light.

But Darin held her fast. Using the pad of his thumb, he gently touched a spot on her cheek while his lips turned down in a deep frown. The hurt look in his eyes made Rylie wonder if he what he was rubbing was dirt or a bruise. As far as she could tell she was nothing but one big bruise.

"Come on," Darin said in soft tones. "It's time you met some of my family."

Family? The first crazy thoughts to enter her mind were how sweaty she was and how much she needed a shower before being presentable enough to meet his loved ones. But her very next thought quickly changed channels back to the reality show of her current life.

Darin was still looking at her as if he would love to eat her for breakfast, much like a man on a first date who was smitten. But their situation seemed to her to be more a life-and-death matter and not much like any date.

Still seething, Hamad Taj Zabbar sat back on the hotel's settee and threw a final instruction to his idiot cousin. "This time, catch up to her without one of the Kadirs nearby. And I don't care how you arrange it, but I expect you to make it look like an accident or a generic kidnapping. And for Allah's sake, take off that damned Taj Zabbar head scarf. I don't want any bystanders putting two and two together. Got it?"

The cousin visibly trembled but stood at attention. "Yes, my sheik. I will not fail again."

At that moment, Hamad received a new satellite call, coming from one of the other Taj Zabbar elders.

Predicting this call would not add a lot to his frustration level, he knew the coming conversation was bound to annoy him in far different ways.

He waved off his dullard of a cousin and waited until the man headed for the elevators. They had already decided Darin Kadir must eventually return to his rooms, and the best plan was to continue following him. He would lead them once again to the woman.

As soon as the cousin was out of sight, Hamad acknowledged the caller.

"A communiqué is being couriered to you," the elder, Mugrin Bin Abdul Taj Zabbar, told him over the line. "Information within the document is classified and vital. Much too vital to send via any modern communication system. Telephones and computers are inadequate. No one must be allowed to waylay these secrets."

The elder paused after speaking, breathing hard into the phone line until he could whisper once again. "We have written the message down using ancient family codes. You will have no trouble translating, I'm sure."

Hamad refused to let any hesitation show in his voice, at least not in the way paranoia clearly showed in the elder's voice. The elder Mugrin could someday be his rival for power. But upon further reflection, that seemed not highly likely. This particular elder was part of the old guard and refused to accept modern technology. How quaint, and yet how annoying.

"No trouble," Hamad said to calm the old man and make him believe all was well. "And will it be left in the usual place and in the usual manner?"

"Of course." Mugrin Bin Abdul sounded worried, and that made their conversation disturbing. Hamad felt certain the elder was concerned about losing his position of power. The man was weak.

Bidding goodbye to the elder Mugrin, Hamad swallowed the dregs of his bitter Middle Eastern coffee, then rose from his shadowed corner spot in the hotel lobby. As he moved, he made slight adjustments to the plans in his mind. He still had time before daybreak to issue new orders.

These new orders would mean a couple of stops and a new final destination for his not-too-bright cousin. But Hamad was certain even Taweel should be able to follow revised instructions. After all, the cousin knew he had but one chance left to make things right, or there would be no chances left for him to have a future. Hamad did not have time to coddle inept employees.

"But why did you bring her here?" Shakir set his jaw and flicked his thumb toward the closed bathroom door where the noise of running water made it clear Rylie was taking a shower. "She could be leading the enemy right to us."

Darin wanted to say that he would never leave her out in the cold and unprotected—this woman of his obsession. He wanted to tell Shakir that nothing his family could say, and certainly nothing she could possibly do, would change their destiny. It was written in the stars.

But he didn't mention any of that. "She's an innocent bystander, bro. The Taj Zabbar came after her, and I think we need to find out why."

"Innocent my ass." Shakir jammed his fists on his hips and the muscles around his eyebrows tensed. "I'm not buying that. What's she doing here in Geneva, anyway?"

Darin turned his back on his middle brother and walked to the sitting room bar. "You won't believe it. She says she came to find out who is responsible for that explosion in Houston. She doesn't think it was an accident. Sound familiar?"

"I bloody well don't accept such a ridiculous excuse. And I can't believe you could be so gullible. What has she done to you?"

Darin straightened his spine without turning around. "She hasn't done anything to me. But you should've seen her take on that Taj Zabbar gorilla without as much as pepper spray to defend herself. She was magnificent."

"Oh?"

Darin felt the air rustling and knew his brother had moved close behind him. He busied his hands with pouring them both drinks, unready to put on his I'm-not-infatuated face. Shakir was the one brother of the three who had been in love, and it had ended badly nearly four years ago. Since then, Shakir had soured on love and women in general.

"I'm calling Tarik," Shakir said through gritted teeth when he reached his side. "When it comes to spy work, he's the most knowledgeable. He can be here by tomorrow evening. Then we'll see what he thinks of all this."

Darin turned and offered Shakir a shot of Blue Goose vodka on the rocks. Though he seldom drank alcohol, his own drink was twenty-year-old scotch. Both of them needed a moment.

Shakir swallowed his down in two huge gulps, then set his ice-filled glass back down on the counter with a slap. "This is the first time any of us has as much as set eyes on one of the Taj Zabbar. I think it must prove the elders have been right all along. We *are* in an undeclared war with them. And you uncovered the truth. You can be proud, brother."

Darin heard the *but* coming loud and clear. "And...?" He urged Shakir to finish the thought.

Shakir lifted a shoulder, dropped it and his chin and glared down at his empty glass on the counter. "And I think it's time you went back to headquarters and began strategizing in earnest. I'm sure the Kadir elders will want you to head up the family's defense systems from now on. Let Tarik and me take care of this first skirmish."

Chuckling into his own drink, Darin lowered his glass and said, "And what do you propose I do with Rylie? Pack her off to America with a pat on the head and no explanations?"

"Works for me. Why not?"

"Because you don't know her. She would never accept leaving without learning the real reason for the attack."

Shakir swiveled to face him. "Oh, and you know her so well after a mere twenty-four hours?"

His brother might have had a point if he'd been dealing in real time. But to Darin, Rylie was the embodiment of the best of his past and his dream of the future. However, he was not ready to voice those feelings, especially not to this brother.

"I think she's in real danger, Shakir. What's to stop them from coming after her in America or anywhere else?"

"Why?" Shakir grumbled under his breath. "The

Taj Zabbar have no quarrel with the Hunts. Last night's attack, if it was for real, and the one in Houston, too, had to be because of us. Because a Kadir was in the vicinity. Have you considered that if she's as innocent as you say, she might be better off—safer—if she stayed away from the Kadirs altogether?"

The idea had crossed his mind but he'd pushed it away.

"She is innocent." No question at all and no room for debate. "And she needs protection. I'm not losing sight of her until we figure out what it is the Taj Zabbar wants.

"You and Tarik do what you do best," Darin continued. "And Rylie and I will see what we can find out on our own."

Shakir looked as if he was about to argue, so Darin cut him off. "Don't worry about me, brother. Together, she and I will be invincible."

Rylie awoke with a start. Something, somewhere, had jerked her from the first sound sleep she'd had in months. Rolling on her side, she was surprised to see it was still dark outside the full wall of windows in Darin's hotel bedroom. The lighted dial on the bedside clock read 5:00 a.m., but she was done sleeping for the night. Peace would never come while thoughts and questions stalked through her mind in brilliant colors and scattered pieces.

She dragged herself out of bed and tried to get her bearings, carefully making her way to the bathroom in the dark. Most of last night remained a blur in her mind. She distinctly remembered the run-in with her assailant, giving him the slip and then coming back here with Darin. And she vaguely remembered Darin treating her like some kind of fragile doll, insisting that she take his king-size bed while he slept on the pull-out couch in the sitting room.

Flipping on the overhead light in his bathroom, Rylie winced against the glare and wished she hadn't been looking in the mirror when the room lit up like a night game at the baseball stadium. Her hair was standing straight up on its curly ends. Her eyes had a sunken-in and bruised appearance. What a mess. Had she looked like this last night when she'd met Darin's brother?

No wonder Shakir had treated her so suspiciously. Who could blame him? It would be hard to trust anyone who looked as disreputable as she did at the moment.

She hadn't gotten a good read on Shakir, other than he was loyal to his brother. And that he was big, bigger than Darin—and mean-looking. Or maybe those mean glances were because he seemed convinced she was one of the bad guys. Her. As if.

She pulled Darin's T-shirt up over her head, grateful that he'd offered it after her shower. Her underpants were still hanging over the shower rod, and she was pleased to find them mostly dry when she slipped them on. After splashing water on her face, she squeezed a dab of toothpaste onto her finger and swished it around in her mouth. One of the men's spray deodorant cans sat on a nearby shelf, and Rylie didn't hesitate to use it on her underarms.

Feeling moderately better, she went back to the bedroom but left the lights there turned off. Forced to feel around until she found her clothes and trusty traveling purse over the back of a chair, she sat down to slide her feet into her jeans and boots. A hairbrush would've been a godsend right about then. But as she hadn't been able to cram one into her tiny purse with the passport, phone and wallet, she ran her fingers through her hair and patted it down the best she could.

Rylie took a second to think about what her next move should be. Darin had made a comment at the end of last night about the two of them working together to solve some mystery. But in her mind, the only mystery was whether she should trust the Kadirs. Every time a Hunt found themselves too near a Kadir, all hell broke loose.

Would she dare try it again?

Maybe. Maybe she could try again at some point— just to prove to herself this magic she felt with Darin was for real. It had been a long time since her body had responded to the touch of a man. And it had been even longer…as in never…that she'd wanted a man to hold her and protect her through a long, sleepless night.

Darin Kadir was special. All of a sudden she'd been thinking about a future instead of wishing she had died in that explosion along with her father.

But before they could talk about any kind of future, she had to learn all his secrets. Was he dangerous? Potentially evil? A part of her wanted to wait and ask him for the explanations, trusting him beyond what seemed reasonable for someone she had recently met. But a bigger part, a more thoughtful part, was afraid he could tell her anything and she would never know that he'd lied until it was too late.

Nope. Rylie knew she had to find out about his past, his family's secrets, all on her own. Then when she asked him and he told her the truth, she could be sure he wasn't spinning fancy tales.

With that settled in her head, the only thing left for her to do was to slip out of his hotel suite without being noticed.

Chapter Five

breakfast, and he told her the truth: thought of sure
he wasn't smiling many times

With her snuggled in next to her one night, but he
had to drive to the end of the road and without even
blinked as

Chapter 5

Arms crossed under his head and lying flat on his back on the sofa, Darin stared into the night while lights coming through the glass doors bounced off the ceiling like tiny, ghostly bats. He'd heard the water running in the bathroom and knew it had to be Rylie because Shakir had ducked out at about 3:00 a.m. Grinning absently into the blackness of the room like an idiot, he wondered if it was normal for her to wake at such an early hour.

Everything about her was unknown and fresh. What did she like to eat for breakfast? What kind of scented soap did she prefer? He couldn't wait to begin peeling back the layers and discovering the real Rylie Hunt.

He'd only managed a couple of hours of sleep, but that's all he usually needed. During most nights, his mind raced with plans and schemes—for making money or finding other ways to get ahead in business. Not sleeping through the night wasn't out of the ordinary.

What felt unusual tonight was the way his thoughts had centered on a single woman. He'd never seriously considered becoming involved before. And yet tonight, all he could think about was how to convince Rylie that they should give romance a try.

He wanted to know her—every detail—both mind and body. He wanted to slip into her soul. He wanted to stand beside her during rough times and console her during the darkest nights.

What was the matter with him? Was the woman a witch? In such a short time, how could he be this sure she was what he wanted?

Yes, it was true he loved the way that burnt-cinnamon hair of hers curled lazily upon her neck. And yes, his hands itched to touch her skin every single time they came within ten feet of one another. But were those good enough reasons to make him want to change his whole life?

Logically, no. But nothing about his obsession seemed logical, and that was the rub. He was a man of thoughts, not passions. He was a planner. A man with lists and goals and tomorrows never in doubt. It was bad enough that the Taj Zabbar had unleashed their war of retribution at a critical time in his business life, disturbing his goals. But he'd had no choice in the matter.

He did have a choice with Rylie. He could send her away as Shakir suggested, and perhaps that would be the best for everyone involved. But oh, no, not him. He couldn't even entertain the idea. Not when she needed both his protection and his basic knowledge of the Taj

Zabbar—and not until he found out why he'd become this obsessed.

The last time any emotional subject had captured his entire attention was when he'd been twelve and his mother left. Stopping to shake his head at the wrong choice of word, Darin quickly corrected his thoughts. She had not left—voluntarily. She'd died. The two were not the same thing, though to his twelve-year-old mind they'd felt similar.

Somehow the situation with Rylie felt the same. He remembered only too well the frustration he'd experienced when he hadn't been able to save his mother from the cancer that consumed her. Now his frustration was mounting again as he tried to find the right words to say to Rylie. Words he could say that would be convincing enough for her to let him provide the protection needed to save her life.

The water stopped and Darin wondered if she would be going back to bed or coming out here to the sitting room. He could make a pot of coffee if she wanted to talk.

He hoped she wanted to talk. The thought of seeing her again. Of sitting next to her. Of hearing her voice speaking to him was enthralling. The nervous excitement was almost more than he could stand.

Sitting up abruptly, he chastised himself. Weren't those the sort of thoughts a lovesick schoolboy might have? The adult inside him felt embarrassingly absurd at the idea of such a childish obsession.

Still, ridiculous or not, Darin found he was holding his breath and waiting for her appearance.

In a few seconds the bedroom door opened. But instead

of lights and the sound of Rylie's voice whispering to him and asking if he was awake yet, nothing happened. Then he heard the rustle of her moving through the room and wondered what came next.

Next was the sound of the suite's hallway door being opened from inside. She was sneaking out? Leaving without him?

He rose to his feet and started to call out when the door shut with a quiet snick.

Hurt but determined that she would not rush into possible danger without his protection, Darin quickly slipped a polo shirt on over his head and shoved his arms into his jacket, grateful he still had on his jeans. He grabbed up his passport, money, phone and the gun from the coffee table where he'd dumped them last night. Meanwhile, he'd shoved his feet into his shoes.

By the time he made it to the hallway, the elevator doors were already closing. His suite was on the twelfth floor and Darin headed for the emergency stairs at a run. Fury and fear were equal partners in his chest as he banged down the stairs and, out of breath, crashed through a door into an alcove off the lobby. Checking every square inch of the grand lobby, bar and alcoves in one fluid glance, he turned to the elevators. Soon he realized she must have arrived first and already left through the front door.

But why? And where was she going?

He still refused to accept the idea that she was involved with the Taj Zabbar. Shakir had been dead wrong about that. He had to be.

Arguing the point in his mind, Darin all but flew across the lobby to the main entrance. Outside, the sky ran in streaks of Halloween colors as daybreak made a memorable entrance across the Alps.

"Can I be of assistance, sir?" The uniformed doorman crossed the pavement, coming in his direction. "Will you need a taxi? It's early but…"

"Did a woman just come out and order a taxi? Did you see her?"

The doorman studied him for a second. "You are Monsieur Kadir, yes?"

"Yes. Did you see her?"

"A pretty young woman left the hotel a moment ago, sir, but she did not request a taxi. She asked for directions to the nearest tram stop. I told her that Geneva trams do not run for another hour, but she insisted."

Darin still had a chance to catch up to her. "Which way did she go?"

The doorman pointed and gave him curt directions to the proper corner. Darin threw bills toward him and was gone with the man's thank-you still resounding in his ears.

As his feet pounded down the sidewalk, Darin tried to imagine what would've made her leave without a word. The answer came from a voice in his head, a surprising voice sounding very much like his dead mother's.

Fear would make a woman run. Rylie was afraid. Afraid of what the Taj Zabbar wanted with her, of course. But he also suddenly understood that she was probably a little afraid of him, too. After all, he'd used his usual detached-father-figure attitude. And what did she know of him really?

Don't be afraid.

He wouldn't hurt her, or let anyone else hurt her.

But she had to listen before he could make her understand that.

Give me a chance, Rylie. I'll make everything okay.

Rylie froze in place when she heard footsteps coming from behind her. Shifting to the side, she went into fight-or-flight mode, flattening her back against the nearby building before finally turning to look that way.

Nothing.

Nothing back there but empty shadows cast by dawn's first light. Not one soul was on the street at this hour. Nevertheless, the skin on her arms swam with imaginary insects while her heart raced wildly in her chest. Maybe she'd been unwise to insist on the tram instead of a cab this time.

Fighting off the strong adrenaline rush that had nearly blinded her, Rylie worked to calm her nerves by taking deep breaths. Now that she'd convinced herself no one was really there and it had all been in her mind, she figured it was senseless to worry about being followed at such an early-morning hour. How would anyone know where to look? She had told no one but Marie Claire that she would be staying overnight in Darin's hotel suite.

Grateful that Darin hadn't awoken when she'd sneaked out, Rylie still felt sorry that she hadn't at least said goodbye. She owed him a thank-you for helping to save her from a would-be kidnapper and for giving her a place to crash afterward. Though truthfully, she could've handled the whole situation on her own without anyone's interference, thank you very much.

Sighing, Rylie gave in, knowing she would take time to thank Darin. In person. As soon as she found out more about him and the whole of the Kadir family's history.

She continued her walk down the sidewalk in the growing light, heading for the tram stop and a ride back to the safety of Marie Claire's apartment. Rylie looked up and realized she only had another block to go, then it would be right around the corner to the stop. She was close. Too close to be worried over nothing.

Gazing down the hill between the buildings, she caught sight of the lake bathed in the lavender color of early-morning light. Streaks of gold shone against the water as streams of mist rose like tiny, spewing geysers across a cloud-filled fountain. The unusual sight reminded her how strange the last thirty-six hours had been.

Something odd was happening inside her. She felt different from when she'd first arrived in Geneva.

Rylie took a quick inventory of her feelings while she walked. Grief, her familiar best friend, still hung around her shoulders, quietly threatening at any moment to bring her stumbling to her knees. And the dogged determination to find truth continued its own kind of bubbling irritation unabated in her chest. Sometimes that stubborn determination made it difficult for her to breathe. But at least those two things remained the same.

So what felt different?

As she continued the debate in her mind, Rylie turned the final corner—and ran smack into a bulky, bug-eyed man with a huge frigging knife in his hand.

Ohmygod. Ohmygod. Ohmygod.

Her feet were stuck to the concrete. Her tongue

swelled up to twice its size. Terrified, she couldn't run or scream.

"You will come now, Miss Hunt." It was the same voice. The same man from before but without the head scarf.

Rylie had never in her memory been at a loss for words. But this time, when she opened her mouth to either scream or demand the man tell her why he was doing this, nothing came out but a strangled gurgle.

All she could do was stare down at the biggest knife she had ever seen. The damned thing had to be at least eighteen inches long, with a double-edged blade, a leather hilt and what looked like some kind of animal head carved into the metal of the handle. Holy moly. It was an antique dagger, for heaven's sake. Lethal, hooked at the tip and pointed straight at her gut.

She had to do something or die. Screaming was out. Even if she could've managed, there wasn't anyone around to hear.

After taking another quick breath to fill her lungs with fortifying air, Rylie brought to mind the promise she'd made to her father. And the many workouts she'd undertaken in order to be able to take care of herself. Her daddy had seen to it that she knew how.

"Nobody is going to coddle you, little girl," Red Hunt had said as he'd dragged her to self-defense classes and taught her how to shoot a gun. "And nobody will ever take care of you the way you can take care of yourself. Be strong, Rylie Ann. You're a Hunt. We take care of others. We don't wait to be rescued."

But, Daddy, this knife is huge.

"Please seat yourself in the auto, miss," the man

muttered in a deep, gruff tone, scaring her almost beyond her wits.

The devil's words rang terrifying alarm bells in her ears. She turned her head and saw that a car with a driver sat at the curb with its motor running.

Two assailants.

Oh, man. Rylie figured if she was ever going to get out of this, big fat knife or not, it would have to be while she was still outside the car with only one attacker and not two. She remembered learning that your first escape is always your best. *Never get into the car.*

"All right. All right. I'm going." At least she'd managed those words. And they hadn't sounded as horrified as she'd felt. Silently promising her daddy to do her best, she readied her body by going into fight mode in the way she had been taught.

Gathering up every ounce of adrenaline she could, Rylie pretended to turn toward the car while secretly rebalancing her weight. Her legs were shaking, but other than that she felt ready.

When she turned, her assailant turned, too, and put himself at a disadvantage. Now or die.

Her feet exploded from under her body as she kicked out at his knees with such force that she took both of them to the ground. He grunted as he fell on his back, and the knife dropped from his hands.

All Rylie wanted to do was get the hell out of there. She tried scrambling out of his reach. But before she could crawl to safety and get to her feet, he grabbed her with an iron grip around the waist.

She scratched and kicked, trying for the eyes or groin. But he must've had a good forty pounds on her. Out of the chaos, she heard him call to his comrade in a language she didn't understand. But she understood the sentiment. Her assailant was calling for reinforcements.

Oh, Lordy. When it came to two against one, she wouldn't stand a chance.

Darin had been jogging down the sidewalk toward the tram stop, hoping to get there before Rylie boarded a tram and was out of sight. But right before he came to the last corner, he slowed his steps, hesitating to scare her by flying around it blind.

Despite his brother's declarations about her being nothing but trouble, Darin was positive that on the contrary she was *in* trouble and needed his help. It made him wonder what he could possibly say to make her understand.

Rylie had an independent nature. Perhaps too independent for her own good. But in a way, he appreciated that about her. No whining or clinging and begging for help from that woman. And he knew her situation back in the States was dire. But she had never even considered asking for his help.

As he took a few slow steps toward the last corner, he knew that's how he would approach her. They could work together, he would say. They could...

He heard the commotion before he jerked past the building on the corner and could see the worst. Rylie. On the ground and being dragged around by another assailant. Momentarily stunned, he thought perhaps this was the same man as last night. But this time he also saw a second man exiting the driver's seat of a car at the curb and yelling toward his comrade in the Taj Zabbar language.

Fighting hard, Rylie was holding her own with the

bigger man for the moment. His first instinct to run to her assistance would've been all wrong. Right then the second man came around the front of the car, and he had a gun in his hand.

The second guy was so absorbed with the vision of Rylie and her attacker on the ground that Darin had a moment to reach for his own weapon without anyone noticing. He drew the gun from under his jacket and then wasn't sure what to do with it. If he shot at the second man and missed, Rylie might be killed.

Frustrated by indecision, Darin started yelling, raised his weapon and began shooting above the second man's head. With the first gunshot, everyone stopped dead, frozen in their places and staring at him.

That instantaneous silence didn't last long, however. The man standing raised his own gun and turned, pointing it directly at Darin. Looking down the deadly end of a monster gun barrel, Darin knew he had no choice. He dropped his arm and fired before the other guy got off a single shot.

The man with the gun stumbled back when the bullet hit him in the middle of the chest. A bloodstain blossomed at the entry point. So much blood. The man's arms flailed and his fingers loosened from around his gun. He gurgled something incoherent and then crumbled to the ground, his gun skittering off into a gutter.

Stunned by what he had done, Darin was a little slow to turn around, transfixed by a man taking his last breaths. Then a scream broke through his fog. Rylie.

Swinging around, he pointed his weapon at the ground where Rylie and her assailant had last been tumbling together. But Rylie alone remained on the sidewalk. She was screaming at the other man, who was running like his life depended on it and just about to disappear at the end of the block.

"Go after him," she demanded.

Darin shook his head and slid his finger off the trigger. "Let the Geneva police department handle it. Someone is sure to have called them by now.

"Are you all right?" He started toward her but she was on her feet and dusting herself off before he could take two steps in her direction.

"I'm okay. Did you kill that man?" She pointed at the second assailant lying crumpled in the street, and then she went back to brushing off her jeans.

He hadn't wanted to think about that yet. But Darin forced himself to turn and go to the prone man's side. He touched the pulse point found at the base of the neck and felt nothing. Next he leaned in close to the man's face, hoping to feel even a small breath of air coming from his nose. Nothing.

The truth poked its nasty finger in Darin's chest. He had killed a man. A member of the Taj Zabbar clan, most probably. But dead was dead, and the idea pushed reality right in Darin's face with a resounding thud.

Then he spotted something beside the man. Whatever it was that caught his eye gleamed through the last shadows of dawn. The shiny thing had apparently dropped from the dead man's jacket pocket and was glinting irreverently in the first rays of the sun.

Darin reached out and picked it up, wanting closer study. It was a key—with an attached tag and writing in French. The lighting wasn't good enough for Darin to read all the words, but he saw enough to sense that this was a key to a lockbox or locker.

Palming it, he decided it must be important and he wanted to get a better look at it in a good light. Some sixth sense was telling him this key could provide the Kadirs with a few answers. And he wasn't about to let loose of it until he found out what.

"Did you find something?" Rylie tilted her head, and when he didn't answer right away, began walking toward him.

Vibrating sounds of Swiss police sirens began jangling, interrupting the still morning air. Both of them stopped and turned their heads to the noise. Judging from how loud it sounded, the police would be there any second.

Darin looked over at Rylie. He was torn, but knew the police could take good care of her. Nothing bad would happen if he followed his hunch now and left her behind.

It wouldn't be forever. He vowed to catch up to her later in the day. They still had much to discuss.

Backing down the sidewalk in the other direction, he yelled, "I need to run this down." Then he picked up his pace. "You stay and talk to the police. Tell them the truth. I'll let you know what I find out."

With that, he turned, darted across the street and disappeared around a corner before she could utter the first word.

Be safe, Rylie. I will see you soon.

Chapter 6

It took Rylie a moment to close her gaping mouth. Darin left. He actually ran off and left her with a dead body, the police on the way and with no real explanations for what had taken place.

"Tell them the truth," he'd said.

Dang it. What truth? That one man had attacked her and then disappeared? And that another man saved her and then he, too, disappeared? Not cool. She could end up spending the rest of the year in a Geneva jail before it was all straightened out.

She turned her head, blankly looking in the direction of the screaming sirens. Indecision wrapped her in a blanket of anger.

How could he leave? And what did he find that was important enough for him to, quote: "Run this down"?

Not a chance in hell you're leaving me behind, pal.

Taking a quick look around at the scene, Rylie made sure her travel purse was still under her shirt before considering both the knife and the dead man's gun. But she had no place to carry either one. So, throwing up her hands and cursing all men under her breath, she took off in the same direction as she'd seen Darin run.

She had always been a fast runner. On the track team in high school, and she'd placed in the state college finals in the one hundred. She figured Darin's leather-soled shoes would slow him down on the still-damp streets.

When she first rounded the corner, Rylie discovered she was right. And lucky. She spotted him as he was dashing around another corner on the next block up.

With sounds of sirens blaring in her ears, Rylie ran to that corner without hearing a single sound that resembled a bystander's shout. Regulating her breathing in preparation for another sprint, she prayed no one had spotted her leaving the scene. But it was too late now for any such regret. Her decision to leave was already made.

Ducking into the shadows of the same deserted alley where Darin had disappeared, she had to slow her steps and hug the building the moment she spotted him standing in the sunshine of the upcoming street corner. Should she confront him now? Maybe not. She decided against it for the time being because she was afraid he would only give her the slip again.

He was paying her no mind and seemed to be concentrating on something in his hand. No doubt the object he'd found near the dead man. What was it?

Once again, she found herself cursing him under her

breath. He'd said he wanted to protect her. That the two of them could work together. Well, hell. Leaving her to fend off the police on her own and then taking a potential clue with him to study didn't seem like ways for someone to earn trust.

Who was this guy, anyway? One second he was all responsible and proper. The next friendly and sexy. Now he was acting like a double agent in a spy movie. The man was driving her crazy.

Dying to run him down and demand answers, she held back. She could no doubt catch him again if he took off. But maybe she should stay here a moment and then follow, see where he went?

He reached into his pocket right then, pulled out his cell phone and made a call. And in the end it was curiosity that decided her question. He promptly hung up and checked around as if he were trying to get his bearings and make sure no one was following.

Where to now, Darin "the Sneaky"?

Glancing over his shoulder, he apparently decided he was in the clear and turned down a street that was now steeped in brilliant sunlight. Rylie wasn't about to lose him after everything that had happened. She ran full out until she, too, hit sunshine. Then she came to a screeching halt, looking in every direction for which way he'd gone.

But he was nowhere in sight.

Rylie pushed off, hoping she'd guessed right and moving as fast as she dared on the suddenly crowded sidewalks. Morning traffic and pedestrians heading for work all conspired against her. She excused herself as she tripped over an older woman who had stopped to gaze in a window. Then Rylie had to step into the busy street in order to get out of the way of a baby stroller being pushed by a heavyset woman.

Growing rash, Rylie deliberately landed in the street and began jogging down the gutter. If Darin had gone the other way or turned off somewhere, it might be hopeless trying to find him in the bustling city. But try she would.

Stopping at the next street corner to catch her breath, she looked up—and there he was. She'd only had a glimpse but was sure that had been his polo shirt she'd spotted as he'd turned into one of the stores or apartments in the next block.

Rylie waited for a bus to pass by, then walked swiftly to within ten feet of the same spot where she'd last seen him. She was beginning to feel like a really bad covert operative. Nevertheless, she flattened herself to the wall before easing her head around the corner to check it out. She found an entrance to a stairwell. It held open stairs leading up to offices above the stores.

And the stairwell was empty. Narrow stone stairs led up into the darkness above. Checking out a posted signboard at the bottom of the stairs, she tried to guess which office would be the one where he'd been headed.

Her French was so poor that she couldn't make out the meanings on a couple of the signs. But she felt sure one of them was listed as a doctor's office. Another sign read: Émigré Europe Ltd. And in smaller letters below that, it said something about business services for foreigners. Darin was a foreigner here.

But had he gone to that office? Or maybe to the doctor? And if so, why?

Unsure what to do next, Rylie came to the conclusion that her best bet would be to wait. Find a place close by where she could stake out the sidewalk entrance and hang around there until he came out. She would give him an hour, no more. Then she would go upstairs and start pounding on doors until someone told her something—or until someone called the police.

Wishing he had more knowledge about covert operations, Darin wondered how to charm the middle-aged woman behind the counter. She was making every effort to speak in English, though Darin would have preferred French to her broken, stilted, one-sided conversation.

"*Oui*, monsieur. We pride ourselves on our security. No one would be allowed access to your depository box but you yourself."

In the strictest terms, she was not correct, since in truth this wasn't Darin's box at all. Nor had the woman's statement been an answer to his original question. But he was not about to force understanding on this woman when she was trying so hard to be accommodating.

Murmuring a thank-you in both languages, he bowed slightly and made his way, at her invitation, behind the counter to a half-hidden row of safety boxes located in the back alcove of the divided room. Émigré Europe Ltd., as written on the key, had turned out to be a moving and forwarding company, with offices located all over Europe. They helped businessmen and their families relocate to various cities on the Continent.

Not only did they provide furniture and possessions moving and storage for corporate employees on a temporary basis, they also served as a mail-forwarding concern. And the key he'd picked up was for one of their lockboxes. Émigré Europe did not seem to have an adequate security system in place to ensure the right person picked up mail.

Using the key he'd found to open the matching numbered box, he withdrew a medium-size leather portfolio. The tooled leather was quite old. Several centuries old, if Darin was any judge. He noticed a unique symbol in the pattern etched into the leather. The panther. The ancient Taj Zabbar family symbol, meant to signify any marked object as belonging to their clan leaders.

Checking over his shoulder to see if anyone was watching, Darin carefully opened the portfolio. Inside, he discovered a five-by-six packet of papers, all strung together like a notebook and then secured with twine. Interesting. He sneaked a peek at what was written on the pages but couldn't make out the language at first glance. Besides the packet, he also found a half-page note, handwritten in the Taj Zabbar language, and two one-way tickets on this afternoon's train to Milan.

Torn between replacing the portfolio in the box and waiting to see who might come to pick it up or instead taking the whole portfolio with him for further study, Darin decided the better choice was to get the hell out of there as fast as possible. He was too curious to hang around. Plus, getting caught here would, more than likely, not be good for his health.

He jammed all the contents back into the portfolio, relocked the box and left with the whole leather packet under his arm. Once outside he would find a quiet place to give everything another look.

The moment Darin hit the sidewalk at the bottom of the stairs, he heard police sirens—and they seemed to be coming in his direction. Had someone turned him in for the shooting? How would they have found him? For security's sake, Darin never hesitated. He took off at a dead run, brushing past noonday shoppers and crashing through lunchtime crowds.

Ten blocks later he was out of breath, but the sirens had long since faded into the city's bustle. Luckily, he found an empty table in an out-of-the-way open-air café. Sitting, he ordered bottled water and surreptitiously checked the people sitting at other tables drinking morning coffee. He had that same strange feeling that someone was watching him again. But he couldn't find anyone staring, or even glancing in his direction.

After his water arrived, Darin felt a little calmer. No one could possibly be following him. He had been careful.

Opening the portfolio and spreading the contents on the table, he fingered the paper pamphlet and flipped through its pages. What sort of language was this? It looked like some kind of ancient Sanskrit writing, but Darin didn't believe that could be true. The paper was modern. Cheap. Bought at any store.

Certainly someone in the Kadir family organization would be able to translate this. Perhaps his cousin Karim would like to take a stab at it. Karim was the computer genius in the family, and also an amateur cryptologist. He should have no trouble figuring out the meaning of these words—if they were real words.

Darin put down the pamphlet and opened the note, handwritten in the Taj Zabbar language. He'd been taught the language as a boy and wondered if he remembered enough of their grammar to translate this message.

The writing on the note was scratchy, hurried. But he made out enough of the words to understand. It was clearly a note from one of the Taj Zabbar elders to an underling.

After bumbling through a few more passages, Darin could see he would need help—and now. Pulling out his satellite phone, he dialed his brother Tarik, who answered before the first ring.

Quickly telling his youngest brother the gist of what he'd been through thus far, Darin went on to add the facts of what he now had in his possession.

"Bring it to headquarters," Tarik said gruffly. "I hope that pamphlet is as important as it seems. We could stand a break in our covert war of innuendo with the Taj Zabbar. Plus, you should be off the streets and out of sight as soon as possible."

Tarik cleared his throat and added, "You've never had to kill a man before, have you?" Not a real question, as Tarik already knew the answer. "Maybe you need to talk about that with someone. Taking a life can lead to serious personality and emotional changes. Come back to headquarters and…"

"I'm all right. I don't need any help." Though Darin did feel changed. "There's too much to do here. I'll go back there in a few days when all this calms down." And after he'd had a chance to explore his obsession with Rylie.

"Not in a few days," Tarik demanded. "Now. I suspect you have the Geneva police, the Taj Zabbar *and* that Hunt woman all looking for you. Get off the streets now."

Darin wasn't quite ready to hide. "I will. But I sincerely believe someone should follow up on this note first. It appears to be an order for one of the Taj Zabbar soldiers to bring both the pamphlet and Rylie to an address in Milan by tomorrow afternoon for a meeting. Two tickets for the sightseeing train leaving Geneva CFF station in an hour were included. I want to be on it."

"You? No. You bring us the papers and we'll take it from there." Tarik's American-accented words were spoken with a hoarse rasp, and Darin heard his sincerity through the receiver. It seemed his baby brother was every bit as concerned for his safety as Shakir had been.

When Darin didn't respond, Tarik became all the more insistent. "Why the need to travel by train? I can fly to Milan and be there by noon tomorrow with skilled men and covert equipment. Let us handle this the right way."

Darin held the phone between his shoulder and his ear, checking the time and waving at the waiter, yet still trying to make his brother understand. "I'd be willing to bet a cool grand that Taj Zabbar henchman, the one who ran away after this morning's assault attempt, may still try to make the train. Or maybe, at least make the meeting tomorrow in Milan.

"And, brother," Darin added, "let me tell you that I can't wait for another opportunity to question that son of a snake."

Still seeing in his mind's eye the man with his hands all over Rylie, Darin drew in a breath and made another urgent request of his baby brother. "Send someone to the Geneva police to rescue Rylie as soon as you can, will you? The Kadirs' fight with the Taj Zabbar has nothing to do with her. But I will find out what they wanted with her. Tell her I'll take care of it, and that I'll contact her as soon as I can." ·

Through the phone, he could hear Tarik grinding

his teeth before he said, "Listen, I'll make a few calls on Rylie's behalf, but I can't shuffle anyone to Geneva in time to take that train today. Though I promise to personally be at that meeting in Milan tomorrow.

"You got us a decent lead there, oh brother of mine," Tarik said with real appreciation in his voice. "Just don't screw things up now, and don't take any unnecessary chances. Stay off that train. Pocket the pamphlet and leave Geneva on the first flight out."

The waiter arrived with his check, and Darin threw a few bills on the table as he dashed to the curb to hail a taxi, still holding the phone to his ear. "Sorry, you're fading in and out," he lied. "I'm going to Milan. Take care of Rylie for me."

Before Tarik could remind him that satellite phones did not fade, Darin shut down his phone and slipped into a waiting taxi.

Rylie had to run full out from her hiding place beyond the potted plants in order to catch up to Darin. But he was in a cab and gone before she could get his attention. She'd wanted to wait until he was off the phone and then appear out of the crowds at his table side and demand to know what was going on.

Terrified at the thought of losing sight of him before she could badger him into explaining, she hailed a cab and got lucky for once as one stopped at her feet.

"Can you follow that cab?" she asked the driver while diving into the backseat.

Unfortunately, her luck flew right back out the window and landed in the midst of the busy streams of traffic on the street ahead as the driver said, *"Je ne comprends pas ce mot."*

Oh, no. "You don't speak English?"

"*Oui,* mademoiselle. I speak a little."

Rifling through her memory for the right words became nearly impossible when every nerve ending was urging her to be on the way before Darin's cab disappeared. "*Suivre!*"

Hoping she'd used the verb "to follow" and not a way of saying "I'm on a diet," she frantically threw her arms toward Darin's cab and simply ignored any possible embarrassment. "*Je te suis...uh...le taxi!*"

The driver turned to stare where she pointed and pointed himself. "*Ce taxi?*"

"Yes. Please. *Dépêches-toi!*" Wow. Some of her French had come back. The phrase to say "hurry up!" must've been stuck in her mind for all these years. How about that?

The driver nodded, turned back to his steering wheel and eased into traffic about three vehicles behind Darin's cab. She prayed her luck would keep holding for long enough that they wouldn't lose him—and that the driver really understood what she wanted him to do.

She leaned her elbows over the back of the front seat and tried to keep Darin's cab in sight. Fortunately, the traffic was traveling at a snail's pace.

After a few minutes, her driver followed the other cab and turned left onto a street she recognized. Rue de Lausanne was a fairly big street in the downtown section of Geneva and she'd already been here a couple of times in the last forty-eight hours.

The driver made a right turn then and commented in French about something, but she didn't catch his meaning. "Pardon?"

"It goes...*le train,* mademoiselle."

What? "Oh, you mean the taxi is going to the train station?"

"*Oui.*"

What in the heck was Darin up to? She knew he had found or taken something from that office back there. She'd seen him carrying a package that looked like an envelope under his arm. And then he'd been studying something at the café before he made that phone call.

Curiosity was driving her to distraction. She could barely keep her mind on where she was and what she was doing.

Her cabbie pulled in close behind Darin's, already stopped at the curb in front of the station. Rylie fumbled around in her waist purse, digging out enough in traveler's checks to pay her fare. By the time she was done, Darin's cab was pulling away from the curb and Darin was nowhere in sight.

Oh, no. She couldn't lose him now. Taking off at a dead run, she headed for the station's ticket booth. Darin would have to buy a ticket if he was going anywhere, wouldn't he?

But when she finally located the ticket seller, Darin was still out of sight. Now what?

Still breathing hard from her run, she began a slow turn, trying to glance in every corner of the station at once. Halfway around, she came to a dead halt.

"Hi." Darin stood right behind her. Close enough for her nose to almost touch his chin, a giant grin creasing his normally sober face.

Speechless, she reached out and touched him to be sure he was really there.

The moment her hand landed on his chest, Darin pulled her closer, bent his head and planted his lips on hers. Hard and demanding at first, his kiss soon became slow and urgent as she opened for him and their tongues met and tangled. She molded herself to him, their legs aligned and his already hard erection settled in against her belly. Her hands went to his hair. Flames of sensual need licked at her mind, making her totally brainless.

She lost track of time and place. Nothing mattered but the sweet sugar of his mouth and the pure heaven of the hot, wet way he made her feel.

Then a noise came from somewhere outside her fog. She heard someone cough behind her, and the foreign sound broke the mood and pulled her out of Darin's arms fast.

Words came tumbling out of her mouth in a rush. "What do you think you're doing?" As far as smart retorts went, that one left a lot to be desired. But it was far better than either the cuss words *or* the words of desire backing up on her tongue.

A dazed look came and went in his eyes. Finally he said, "I might ask you the same thing. Why are you following me? And what happened with the Geneva police?"

Gulping in air and willing her racing heart to slow, Rylie fought with her own anger and embarrassment and promised not to smack him upside the head for being stupid. "I didn't wait for the cops to show up. Why did you leave me back there and run away?" And where were the words she needed to hear about that spectacular kiss?

His pleased expression, the one similar to the fox who'd just made off with the eggs, disappeared and was replaced by flaring nostrils. "I didn't *run away*. I told you I needed to check something out. And I was concerned that explanations to the police would be too long and complicated."

"Exactly. That's why I followed you. I didn't want to stay, either. And do what? Try explaining a dead body with a gunshot wound, no shooter—and also no gun." Dang Darin's ornery hide anyway.

"You…followed me? All day?" Darin's face flushed red and his eyes narrowed as they shot darts of fury in her direction. "But I stopped a couple of times. Why didn't you say something? Why did the cab driver have to tell me your cab was following us before I knew you were anywhere around?"

"I tried. Or at least I thought about trying a couple of times. But you…"

An announcement of train schedules came across a loudspeaker at that moment. First in French and then again in English and Italian.

"I have a train to catch," Darin told her when the announcement was finished. "Go home, Rylie. All the way home to Texas. My family will help you reach there safely. I'll contact you first chance I get and we'll talk. Explanations can wait till then."

He was shooing her away? Like a fly? And after just kissing her breathless?

"Not a chance, pal. Where you go, I go. Get used to it."

Chapter 7

"Turn back. This is no game." Darin folded his arms across his chest and tried his best glare. He couldn't let her set foot on the train. It was far too dangerous.

Rylie flicked her wrist at him. "Don't be such a jerk. If you're taking the train, so am I." She punctuated each word with a wave of her hand. "I want to know what's really going on."

His brother's warning had been repeating in his head for the last two hours: *"…if she's as innocent as you say, she might be better off—safer—if she stayed away from the Kadirs altogether."*

As obsessed with her as he was, he still couldn't allow her to follow him into a potential trap. And he *was* obsessed. No doubt about it. He'd been positive that kissing her would break the spell. But no. The kiss had only made things worse. He hadn't wanted to stop.

He would have given anything, including his life, for a chance to continue on with that kiss.

Now he would give anything to run away with her to some far corner of the earth. The two of them could explore each other at their leisure. Time. They needed more time.

But they had no time. And at this moment, nothing on earth mattered as much as keeping her safe. Not a covert war. Not his extended family—or even his brothers. Nothing.

She stood there, hands on hips and blue eyes flaring. Magnificent. Her whole body radiated unleashed energy. He'd foolishly indulged himself with that one kiss as a spur-of-the-moment thing. But he hadn't been able to help himself. Her face had been flushed from running, her chest heaving, and his mind had gone blank. The draw of her lips had been a magnet pulling on his libido.

His mind was perfectly clear now. She was in danger, and yet all he wanted to do was kiss her again. To lose himself and all his family's troubles in the depths of her rosy mouth and soft body.

He dug his fingers through his hair. "Rylie, listen to me, please." His own voice was thick with need and shook with fear—for her. "I'm trying to save your life. I could be walking into a trap. The Taj Zabbar..." What could he say to make her understand that all he wanted was her safety?

Those beautiful blue eyes went dark, then shot dangerous daggers of fire in his direction. "Just one minute, bub. After everything we've been through in the last couple of days, do I strike you as the timid type? As some kind of fragile flower?"

She fisted her hands; opened and closed them. It was as if he could read her frustration. He could see that she was strung tight with it and her tenuous control matched his own. The idea of them being so much in tune was sensual. Almost erotic. The sight of her bouncing on her toes, ready to fight, made him weak in the knees.

She punched him square in the chest. "Well, not *this* Texas Rose. If you're danged determined to take a train, you'd better get aboard. I'll be right behind you. We can talk there."

He opened his mouth to try again. Or to demand that she pay attention to his warnings. Or to…

Right then something in a far corner of the station caught his eye. A man. Standing half-hidden behind a pillar and watching them. The thing that had first caught Darin's attention from across the room—the one thing he most feared—was a purple-checked head scarf of the Taj Zabbar.

Hell.

That changed everything. Darin couldn't possibly leave her here now. At their mercy? And all alone?

"Fine," he said gruffly as he grabbed her by the wrist and twisted them both in the direction of the distant train platform. "Let's go."

Racing for the huffing train, he pulled a stunned Rylie in his wake like a water-skier. The Taj Zabbar had spotted her. Nowhere was safe from their threat anymore. Darin came to a quick decision. Real safety for her would come only if the two of them stayed together.

His original impulse had been the correct one. The two of them had to be attached at the hip from now on.

Regardless of the consequences to his body and soul.

Hunched down on the tufted and cushioned bench of their luxury first-class cabin, Rylie listened to the clack, clack, clack of the train's wheels against the rails. She'd been staring at the quilted wallpaper and sulking since they'd pulled out of the station. Meanwhile, Darin was feigning sleep in the seat beside her.

The package he'd been carrying most of the morning, the envelope or whatever, was nowhere in sight. She'd tried to see if he had the thing on him still, but he never let her get close enough.

He hadn't told her anything so far, either. He'd hustled them onto the train and into his reserved cabin. Next thing she knew, he'd closed his eyes and was snoring. She wasn't even positive she knew where they were headed, let alone the reason for this unexpected trip—or for Darin's sudden change of heart about letting her come.

But she'd taken notice of how he carefully locked the door to their cabin as the train pulled out of the station. Rylie didn't think she could ever forget the look of pure fear that had crossed Darin's face as he'd changed his mind and dragged her across the train station's concrete floor at a sprint. Something—or someone—had scared him into bringing her along.

Squirming in her seat, she turned to look at his profile. His act of sleeping peacefully only incensed her. Just look at that stunning, stubbled jaw of his. At the perfection of his Roman nose and the long black lashes that lazily touched those sculpted cheekbones. Damn him for making the butterflies churn in her stomach.

Her gaze dropped to the mouth that had already shown he knew more than most about great sex. An urge to kiss those fantastic lips of his again curled tightly inside her belly. But in the nick of time, she remembered that his mouth also knew how to tell great lies.

Darin knew more than he was saying about the explosion that had changed her life. Okay, so she was pretty sure he had not been involved directly. But he *knew* who was and he'd been keeping the information from her.

Rylie leaned over and poked him hard in the ribs with her elbow. "Stop pretending to sleep. Get up and talk to me."

"Huh?"

"Don't you *huh* me, Darin Kadir. You're not sleeping for real, and I have a lot of questions. The first one is—where are we headed?"

Darin had the nerve to yawn. "Um…this train is the sightseeing train that travels over the Alps to Milan, Italy. We should be there by midmorning."

"Overnight sightseeing? What can you see in the dark?"

He straightened up. "Wait until you see the beautiful sunsets and sunrises in the Alps this time of year. And the train makes stopovers in Bellinzona and Morithy. Both splendid places for sightseeing. Even in the early morning."

Pursing her lips and narrowing one eye, she said, "Okay, then. But why? Why the heck are we taking a perfectly *splendid* train ride right now?"

"We had the tickets."

Argh. Heaven save her from smart-assed men.

"Can we just talk for a while?" Maybe casual conversation would get to the truth. "My nerves are shot after that assault this morning and from chasing you around all day. I need to settle down."

"Why don't you try a nap?"

Frustrated, she poked him the ribs again. "I can't sleep yet. And neither can you. Don't lie."

He mumbled something she was glad not to hear and then breathed a deep, mournful sigh. "Fine. What do you want to talk about?"

She wanted to ask about the object he'd found, or talk about that horrible, life-changing explosion. But she knew he would only feed her a bunch of bull about those things. So she tried a different tack.

"It was nice meeting your brother. I don't have any siblings myself. Do you have other brothers and sisters?"

"Nice? Shakir would hate being called nice." Darin chuckled and a loving gleam entered his eyes. "I have two brothers. Shakir, whom you met, and our baby brother, Tarik. Only, Tarik would have my head if he heard me referring to him as anything but a tough ex American Special Forces officer."

"Ex? What does he do for a living now? Tell me about him. Tell me about both of them."

Darin cleared his throat. "They're family." His sentence had ended abruptly, as if that was all that needed saying.

But as she was about to ask another question, Darin continued, "Our mother died when I was twelve. Shakir was ten then, and Tarik was five years old. Our father... our father is a very busy man. Besides being head of the board of directors for most of the Kadir family holdings, he is also the titular head of elders in our extended family."

"You mean like a king?"

"Not exactly. I come from a long line of traders and nomads, remember. Because we have no country of our own, the modern Kadir family holds together like a corporation. We own property in various places throughout the world. We own businesses and homes, hospitals and schools. But we don't claim any territory, and we communicate through family reunions and conferences instead of through edicts."

Darin stood, checked the lock on the door, then he sat back down.

"Tell me more about your brothers." She thought about Shakir. At least six-four, he had a quiet intensity about him and an underlying strength that seemed almost chilling.

"I had to step in to be a father figure for them. But I'm afraid I was not in good enough psychological shape at that point to even help myself. Our mother's death hit us all hard.

"Shakir maybe worst of all." Darin shook his head as painful emotions fluttered in his eyes. "Before six months had passed, Shakir began to stutter. He quit his athletic endeavors and buried himself in books."

Rylie had seen something quite different in Shakir from the shy bookworm his brother was describing. A lethal intelligence gleamed in Shakir's eyes, true. But the looks he gave her were more those of a deadly assassin. A man with no morals. A man who would sooner slit your throat than look at you twice.

"If it hadn't been for our maternal grandfather

taking him under his wing," Darin went on, "I'm afraid Shakir might never have broken out of his self-imposed cocoon."

"Oh? I'm glad the rest of the family stepped in to help."

Darin shook his head sharply. "Don't be so quick. Our grandfather was not a man you would've liked to meet in a dark alley. My mother came from a tribe of savage desert warriors, and her father was determined to turn at least one grandson out like his ancestors. Shakir was vulnerable to the mind-bending lessons he received in fierce warfare. He learned a great deal, but none of it is particularly helpful in civilized society."

"He seemed civilized." Just barely.

"Shakir attended a proper English university when he came of age. But then he joined an English paratrooper regiment and spent several years fighting in the isolated mountains of Afghanistan. If he seemed civilized to you, it's only a veneer. Underneath…I'm not too sure what lurks underneath that thin veneer these days.

"But I love my brother," Darin added with a cheerless smile. "Both of them. And the Kadir family is nothing if not loyal. We would all give our lives for each other."

Darin stood again and paced the small cabin. Rylie folded her hands in her lap. This wasn't getting her any closer to finding out what the object was that Darin had found or why they were on this train.

"What about your other brother? You said his name is Tarik?"

"Yes, the baby of the family." This time it was a genuine smile that spread cheer across Darin's face. "When Mother died, Tarik had to compete for attention. He quickly learned the lesson about catching more flies with sweetness than with bitter vinegar. He became the clown of the family. Or…perhaps a better description is the family's chameleon.

"My youngest brother is a master at hiding his true feelings behind a grin." Darin paused his pacing and stared out the window at the passing scenery for a moment before continuing. "You'd like him. Everyone does."

"You said he'd been in the U.S. Army? Special Forces? What's he doing now?"

Instead of answering her questions, Darin turned to look at her. Really look at her for the first time since they'd been on this train. She came to her feet, not knowing why exactly. But it felt important for her to be closer to him.

He took a step and picked up her hands, tenderly holding them both in his own. "Rylie, we only had our suspicions until the happenings of the last couple of days. But now it looks like the Kadir elders were right."

He winced, as though what he had to say would hurt them both. "Apparently, now that the Taj Zabbar have endless pools of money, they've decided to take revenge on the Kadirs. For real. We're fairly sure now they're taking secretive steps to ruin us. And my father believes if they can't ruin our businesses and reputations, they intend to kill us."

Rylie was shocked, almost speechless. "All this over something that happened five hundred years ago or more. Not really?"

"No," he answered softly. "Not really. It's true that old fight probably didn't make us terribly popular among the Taj Zabbar, but grudges can be hard to hold for centuries. In more modern times, about fifty years ago, the Taj Zabbar began mounting a revolt against their Kasht oppressors. They pleaded with world leaders for help, but…"

Darin's hesitation said more than any words. He didn't want to finish telling her his tale.

"Go ahead. This all happened long before either of us was born. I'm listening."

He gently squeezed her hands. "The Kadir elders of that time were working to spread their influences throughout the world. They had made a deal with the country of Kasht for control of a profitable deep-water port—located in Zabbaran territory."

Darin closed his eyes but he never let go of her hands. "It was greed. Pure and simple. Well, and maybe a little desperation. It's not easy becoming a world shipping power without having your own territory.

"Nevertheless," he went on after opening his glazed eyes, "the Kadir elders used bribery, blackmail and whatever other underhanded tricks they had at their disposal to make sure world leaders ignored the Taj Zabbar's pleas for help."

Dropping her hands, Darin turned his back and finished speaking over his shoulder. "The country of Kasht put down the minor Taj Zabbar revolt with iron fists. Many Taj Zabbar died or were thrown into horrific prison camps. It took them nearly fifty years to recover. So you see, the Taj Zabbar have good reason to hate Kadirs."

He was embarrassed. Chagrined over the poor image he'd had to leave concerning his family. Her heart hurt for him in return.

She took a step and touched his arm. "Darin. Please

look at me. None of this was your doing. It all took place a long time—"

"You shouldn't have come." He spun around in one fast move. "If anything happens to you, I'll never forgive myself."

Before Rylie could catch her breath, Darin took her in his arms and lasered a fierce kiss across her lips.

Hunger. Desperation. Sorrow. Humiliation.

Every combined response from both of them registered with her in that moment. And then he took the kiss deeper, and nothing but the two of them and the searing heat mattered at all.

Darin put everything he had into the kiss. All the obsession. All the anger and fear. He plundered her mouth. Punishing, pleading and devouring at the same time.

Go away, he thought in his mind. *Stay forever,* his heart begged. Kissing her long and hard, and with a demand for possession that scared the hell out of him, he felt her whole being returning the sentiment.

And that scared him even more.

Releasing her, he staggered back, his head reeling and his breath coming in erratic bursts. He stared at her through eyes that had misted over. Her own blue eyes were sharp with emotions and questions. Questions he had no answers for at the moment.

"What was that?" she asked in a raspy voice. "It wasn't…it wasn't just…" She stopped, waving her hand like he should be able to fill in the blanks.

He could. But he wouldn't.

"…a kiss. That was not a simple kiss."

She was right. But he could do nothing more than

stand there like a rooted tree while the sound of the train rumbling against the tracks grew louder in his ears.

"Say something," she demanded. "Tell me I'm right. Or—" she narrowed her eyes at him "—tell me I'm wrong. What the hell is happening between us?"

He couldn't give her an answer. He couldn't even give himself an answer. Not while she was in danger. Not while he didn't know if tomorrow his entire family might be blown off the face of the earth.

Finally he opened his mouth, and the weakest thing he had ever said flew from his lips. "Later. We'll have to talk about this much later."

"But…"

At that moment a faint thud came from right outside the door. Darin put his hand over her mouth and shook his head to keep her quiet.

The door's handle squeaked. Another more metallic sound clanked through the silence.

Darin braced himself and pushed Rylie to the back of the cabin. Holding his breath, he positioned his body at the side of the door. Whoever this was would get a big surprise from him.

And then the handle slowly turned—and the door opened just a crack.

Chapter 8

Aware of his weapon, the weight of it heavy where it sat lodged at his back, Darin opted not to draw it and take any chances with Rylie's life. He could hear her turbulent breathing behind him. Could almost feel the erratic pounding of her heart, beating together with his in double-time.

No, this kind of close-range surprise situation called for the hand-to-hand-type combat he'd learned in defense classes. But it became more than he could manage to stand motionless, waiting while the door slowly opened wider. Adrenaline surges crashed inside his head like waves upon a stormy shore.

In the span between two seconds, Darin made his move. Whirling, he kicked the door open and pinned his assailant. Shoulder driven into the intruder's chest and elbow jammed into his windpipe, Darin drew his knife and rammed it up hard under the man's upraised chin, almost piercing the skin.

"What do you want with us?" he growled in a voice not sounding like his own.

The man choked out an answer that Darin didn't understand. Jerking his elbow from the man's Adam's apple, Darin grabbed one flailing wrist and twisted the assailant around. He drew the man's arm up and pressed that wrist solidly between his shoulder blades, thrusting the man's nose into the wall in the process.

"Ow." The cry came out more like a whimper than a war whoop. "Monsieur. Monsieur. Please don't hurt me. Sorry to disturb you. I...I am ze porter."

"Darin, stop! Don't." Rylie's pleas filtered through the fog of rolling hormones zinging around in his mind.

Dropping his hands and lowering the knife, Darin sank backward and fell against the cushioned bench. "What have I done?"

"It's okay. Everything's okay." Rylie filled her lungs with air and went to the unfortunate porter slumped against the open door. "You're not hurt, are you?"

"No, mademoiselle. I..." The man touched his red nose, straightened his jacket and squared his shoulders. "It was my fault. My responsibility is to knock. But I did not think you were in residence."

The man's Italian accent mixed with his stilted French words and covered most of his shaky tones. Rylie was amazed. If this had been America, the guy would've already been lawyering up and screaming about his rights.

"But we locked the door. Didn't we? How'd you get in?"

The man smoothed his finger across his mustache and

cleared his throat. "There is…how you say? Ze porter's key? If you wish not to be disturbed, you must adjust ze sign which tells to all *occupée*. Yes?" He pointed out a sliding button next to the door.

"I came to make up ze bedding," the porter continued as if nothing had happened and everything was in perfect order. "But I will return later. Do mademoiselle and monsieur wish to view a menu?"

Darin came to his feet, eyes suddenly alert. "No food, but a question. I heard a thudding noise out in the corridor right before you came in. Did you see someone else out there?"

"I passed a gentleman as I entered ze car, signor. Another passenger, perhaps."

"What did he look like?"

"Just a man."

Darin looked frustrated. "But was he dressed differently? Anything outstanding that you remember?"

The porter pursed his lips in thought. Finally he said, "Ze gentleman was dressed like a member of a sheik's party." The porter touched a hand to his bare head and lifted his eyebrows.

"With a keffiyeh? The head scarf? What color? Was it purple?" Darin peppered his questions at the man.

The porter withstood the assault of words and made another curt nod in his direction. "*Sì. Ze colore* it was *porpora*."

Darin shoved a handful of Swiss francs at the porter and sent him on his way. Then Darin picked up the long, stiletto-style knife from where it lay on the floor, flipped it closed and returned it to his pocket.

"Where'd you get something like that?" Rylie asked

as the sharpest frigging blade that she'd ever seen disappeared.

"My brother." He hadn't said which brother, but Rylie was guessing something like that could only belong to Shakir.

Darin's eyes were feverish, glazed. Rylie wanted to help him. She eased down onto the bench and lifted her palm, wordlessly pleading for him to join her.

He sat down beside her, but she could feel the nervous tension stringing his body tight with electric charges.

"Talk to me," she said, using as calm and collected a tone as she could muster.

"About what?"

"Finish telling me what your family is doing about the Taj Zabbar threat."

Darin stared at her a long minute, as though he couldn't believe she would be asking such a thing.

But as she was almost ready to say something else, he said, "My brothers and I have taken leave of our professions in order to flush out the truth. Our family must be prepared for the worst." His voice was rough, hoarse, but finally quiet.

"The Taj Zabbar are known to be secretive," he went on. "Few people in the world know for sure what they're up to, and that's been their operating style for centuries."

She was almost sorry she'd asked. He looked so distraught. So guilty—for no good reason she could see.

"We've also recently learned they're covertly trading in a variety of illegal enterprises." Darin shifted and ran his hands down his arms as if he were cold. "The legitimate money they've made in oil seems to be financing more criminal-style activities with the potential for bigger profit yet. Drugs. Arms dealing and weapons of mass destruction. Human trafficking and slavery. A whole plethora of dirty activities."

When Rylie gasped and widened her eyes at the idea of such nasty and deadly dealings, Darin dropped his chin and stared at the carpeted floor. "I know. It sounds bad. But now that we're sure they're conducting a war of retribution against the Kadirs, I'm afraid my next accusation will sound much worse."

This time it was Rylie who picked up one of his hands and grasped it tenderly between her own. "Go on. Whatever it is, I can take it."

"They're coming after our family like a python, using stealth and power to bring us to our knees and choke the life out of our businesses and destroy our families. The explosion that killed your father and my uncle, nearly ruining Hunt Drilling, must've been a tentative first round in their war against the Kadirs."

"I knew that explosion wasn't any accident."

Darin looked into her eyes, anguish clear in his face. "I'm sorry your family got caught up in something so terrible. But my brothers and I will find the person responsible and make it right. I promise."

"You and your family are trying to uncover the Taj Zabbar's next moves. What will you do then?"

"Turn the information over to the international authorities. The United States. The United Nations. If we make the snake public, we remove the worst of its bite."

"I want to help." Her own words surprised her, but she didn't intend to take them back. "I want to let the whole world know who caused that accident and who should be stopped by whatever means necessary."

Shaking his head, Darin whispered, "It's too dangerous. You shouldn't even be anywhere near us. I'm sure that's why the Taj Zabbar has already tried to kidnap you. Because you've been seen with me.

"You have to stay out of this, Rylie," he pleaded. "It's not your war. Let us do what we must. I promise I'll let the world know the explosion was no accident and who it was that caused it. Give me a little time."

"Let me help." Again she surprised herself with such fervent determination. She would help, she realized. Nothing could stop her now that she knew the whole story.

"No. You have to stay safe. Away from the Kadirs and their enemies. Away from me."

She began to argue. "I'm tougher than you…" But then she looked into his eyes. Really looked. The man was terrified—for her sake. No one but her father had ever been concerned for her welfare. The idea was powerful and potentially life-changing.

She interrupted her revolutionary thoughts to turn the subject around with a coy smile. "Let's talk about all this later. Right now I'm too hungry to continue this discussion. Feed me."

After a quick stop in the compartment's tiny toilet to freshen up, Darin ushered Rylie to the dining car. Eager to go in search of the Taj Zabbar assailant whom he felt sure had boarded the train with them, Darin frantically ran through ideas in his head for a way to keep her safe in the meantime.

"Oh, look at the golden eagle." Rylie pointed out the

window to a large bird, soaring in and out of sunset's shadows on the springtime updrafts.

The waiter seated them at a small table set with white tablecloth and sterling utensils. Rylie still didn't take her eyes off the picturesque sight out the window.

"I never believed anything could be this beautiful."

The train was climbing higher, moving slowly past mountain pines and dwarf spruce. Up ahead the ice-covered Alps with their rose-colored peaks were brushed in a golden glow of the setting sun. They stood like a line of sentinels guarding the Swiss-Italian border.

"Would you like me to order a bottle of wine?" he asked to recapture her attention. "A nice Tuscan cabernet or perhaps one of the Masseto merlots?" Maybe with enough alcohol in her system, she would become sleepy and he could lock her safely in their compartment while he searched the cars for their assailant. Or perhaps the porter could scare up a couple of sleeping pills.

"I'd better not. I don't suppose they have sweet iced tea on this train?"

"I'm sure they don't." His chances of locking her away for safety appeared to be more and more remote.

"My ears just popped."

"It's the altitude. We'll be traveling through the Gotthard Pass a little after midnight and dropping into the Ticino valley a couple of hours later. You'll probably experience the effects of more altitude changes by then."

They ordered dinner and ate a meal of spring veal and gnocchi. Whie she was drinking the espresso he hadn't wanted her to order, Darin realized it had grown late and they were the sole occupants of the car. Maybe it was time to try putting a scare into her. That could make her stay out of his way.

He withdrew the Taj Zabbar letter from his pocket. "Do you see this letter?"

She jerked it from his hand and frowned at what must have looked like jibberish to her. "Is this what you found today? A letter? In the Taj Zabbar language? What's it say?"

"It's an order from one of their elders to one of their soldiers. An order demanding the capture and transportation of you—or your body—to a meeting place in Milan tomorrow."

"Me?" She actually had the nerve to beam at him. "Think of that. I wonder how I got to be so important."

This was not the reaction he had anticipated.

"It's nothing to joke about. They want you dead. These men are beyond dangerous, Rylie. You need to give them a wide berth. We've intercepted messages from them before that tell about torture and seduction of young women for both profit—and for fun. Stay out of their line of sight."

She casually shrugged a shoulder and studied her fingernails.

Finally she glanced up at him. "But what if I *let* them capture me? Couldn't your family use someone on the inside? I could listen for…"

"Not one chance in a thousand hells of that happening."

Rylie folded her arms over her chest. "Maybe we should ask your brothers for their vote."

"That's it." Darin threw his napkin on the table and stood, pulling her along by the elbow.

"You're going back to the sleeping compartment to wait for me. I'm on this train to find that bastard who attacked you. He boarded with us and I intend to capture him and make him talk."

"But…"

"No buts." Darin had had enough. "You can have the gun. And I'll slip the porter money to keep an eye on the corridor and on your door. You should be safe enough."

He inched his arm around her waist and began shuffling her out of the dining car. But the moment her body was pressed to his, their combined heat raced along his veins and landed hot and erotic at the base of his spine.

Impossible. *Not now.* He eased his grip on her and backed away to a more respectable distance. But he kept them both moving forward through the passenger cars.

Rylie never spoke a word. When he gave her the gun and final instructions on how to use it, she glared up at him with a look that could've set fire to a glacier.

"Stay safe," he reiterated while turning his back on that gorgeous but furious face. "And be here when I return."

He took a deep breath and walked out the door, praying all the while that by leaving her alone he wasn't making one of the biggest mistakes of his whole life.

Rylie stared at the back of the closed door, still waiting for Darin's return and to hear him say he needed her help. Ten seconds. Forty. One minute. Two.

Well, dang it.

Okay, she got that he was worried about her. Really

she did. But she'd also hoped he was coming to know the person she was inside. The person who could never in a million years wait around in safety, sitting on her hands while someone she cared about worked to save her life.

Uh-uh. So *not going to happen, Darin.*

It was amazing how close she felt to him after such a short time. How well she knew the real him even with few words spoken between them. How could he care about her and not know her any better than he apparently did?

And he did care for her, she was absolutely positive. Um, maybe his emotions were based mostly around lust, but he did care. She could easily see that in the way he looked at her and in the way he kept demanding that she stay safe.

Her insides were already jumping, raring to follow after him. But she would sit here for one more minute first. To be sure he didn't turn her around in the corridor and find a way to lock her inside their cabin.

Images churned in her mind as she perched a foot over one knee, flapping it up and down in midair with nervous energy. She cared about him, too. More than cared. In fact, what she'd been feeling verged on a once-in-a-lifetime thing.

But was it real? Her emotions had been on such a roller-coaster ride since she'd first set eyes on him that she hardly knew what to think. It had started out with her being sure she hated him. Positive he'd had a hand in murdering her father. Now she knew he was no murderer. Taking a life in self-defense had all but killed him, too.

As the days and hours had gone by, she'd been

experiencing many other feelings toward him. Some she couldn't even name. Lust was right up there on top, of course. But there was so much more.

That last kiss had been...special. It was the kind of kiss that spoke of millions of tomorrows. The extraordinary sort of kiss that brought to mind knights in shining armor about to give up their lives for the woman they loved. A kiss like nothing in her experience.

Love? Not a remote possibility in their case. Darin didn't even know the true her. And would he still care as much if he did? Maybe not. Maybe they came from such differing backgrounds that he would never be able to respect a strong woman. A woman who wanted to stand beside her man and not behind him as they faced life together. A woman like her.

And how did she feel about him deep down? She knew there was a lump in her chest whenever she thought about him. A lump in her chest and a wildly crazy heat at her core. The man seriously turned her on.

Hmm. Perhaps that could be the answer for all her questions. The two of them needed to have sex. That would clear both their minds of any infatuation and prove once and for all if their differing backgrounds could ever be overcome.

Rylie found it easy to imagine that whatever lust Darin had been feeling for her would quickly disappear in a puff of smokin' hormones after one roll in the hay. She'd seen it happen to men before. But she wasn't going to push him into having sex for his sake alone. She wasn't that horny. No, she had come to the conclusion that the two of them should have sex for her *own* enlightenment. She was the one who needed to discover how becoming intimate with a person so different from herself would affect her emotional well-being.

Would she want more? Or would she run screaming from his arms and fly all the way home, glad to be free? She would never know until she tried.

Yep. That was all settled. Having sex was the plan.

But first she had to make sure he stayed alive.

Two hours later Rylie's ears were popping again as she crept through the quiet corridors looking for any sign of Darin or the Taj Zabbar kidnapper. The train must be heading lower, going in the direction of the lake below the mountains. Rylie could almost feel gravity pulling her downward.

She must've been just missing Darin and the kidnapper while she searched. It was possible they had ducked into a cabin or hidden behind a closed door when she'd gone by. But she had traveled the length of this train twice, looking. Now she wasn't sure what was left to…

The train rounded a steep U-curve right then, and Rylie got a good view through the windows into another corridor as the snaking cars doubled back on themselves. There, maybe only two or three train-car lengths ahead, she saw two men locked in mortal combat in the well-lit corridor of a sleeping car.

Darin.

Blasting out of her own corridor at a dead run, Rylie swore under her breath. She should be covering his back. She was the one with the gun, after all.

She pushed through pressurized door locks and tramped across the little vestibules that connected two cars. Through one car. Then into the next.

By the time she hit the third empty corridor in a row she was breathing hard and very confused. She'd seen them. Clearly. It hadn't been a dream.

Then she heard a noise coming from the end of the car. It sounded as though someone had momentarily gone through the pressurized door onto the next vestibule. Shoving hard to open the door, she blinked at sudden air movement and turned her head in that direction.

To her amazement, she saw shoes as they disappeared up a ladder that she'd never noticed before. A ladder to the roof of the train? Why?

After she heard a distant shout, sounding for all the world like Darin's voice, the why didn't seem too important. If he could chase someone to the roof of a train, she could follow.

She carefully checked to be sure the gun was secure in her waistband. Then, shaking her head at the craziness of the whole idea, she began to climb.

A cold blast of wind whipped prickles of ice at her body as she neared the roof's edge. But that didn't stop her. Nothing could've stopped her until she found out what was going on up above.

Peeking over the edge of the roof, she saw a sight that took her breath. Darin and the Taj Zabbar would-be kidnapper battling with each other. One swung wildly and then the other did the same. Both had knives drawn and were swearing at each other in different languages.

Rylie eased her body onto the roof and lay there spread-eagle, wondering if she had the nerve to stand up while the train was traveling on a twenty-degree incline. Then the car leveled out some while the train rolled across a well-lit trestle above a deep, glacial-cut ravine.

She watched as the kidnapper struck out at Darin's hand and his knife flew free. Darin whirled in a defensive move and the kidnapper's knife went sailing, too.

Sucking up courage, Rylie pulled the gun free and came up on her knees and elbows. Pointing the weapon at the kidnapper, she screamed over the roar of the wind.

"Stop! Stand still. I've got you covered."

When Darin turned his head toward her, his face went deathly pale. Before she could blink, he dove in her direction and tried to shield her with his body.

"Here." She thrust the gun at him.

He turned it on the kidnapper, but the man was close and scrambling toward both of them with desperation in his eyes.

Everything seemed to happen at once after that.

Darin fired. Ducking, the kidnapper slipped on a patch of ice and started sliding. Darin reached out, trying to give the man a hand. Rylie watched in horror as the man's fingernails scratched deep grooves in the paint with his futile attempts to stay in place.

And then, without a noise, without any sound at all above the howling winds, the Taj Zabbar kidnapper was gone.

Vanished into the nothingness of the dark night.

Chapter 9

Back in their cabin, Darin and Rylie sat together in silence on the newly made-up bed. Both of them waiting for their heart rates to settle. Grasping her hand to assure himself that she was truly alive, Darin couldn't believe how close he had come to losing her for good.

What was he going to do with her? Part of him was fascinated with her independence and that amazing self-confidence in her own abilities. She stirred something in him in a place that no one had ever reached before.

But another part of him, the more rational and coherent part, was horrified at the chances she took. He could never keep her safe if she kept undermining his efforts at every turn.

But how would he ever manage to talk her into walking away from a fight that was not her own? Darin feared he was partially to blame. He had been keen to keep her close. Secretly dying for a chance of the two of them becoming intimate. He had been positive that having sex with her would disabuse him of his powerful obsession.

A nearly fatal mistake on his side.

He must change all of that—and quickly. His obsession would have to be buried now, without the benefit of seeking out an answer to his questions of why. The real truth to the matter was that they were obviously unsuited. A committed relationship between them would be out of the question. This whole obsession thing had to have been born out of pure lust. And lust could always be conquered by the power of the mind. Or buried by the power of determination.

Yes, things must change. He would find a way to send her away by feigning disinterest. Now that her would-be kidnapper was gone for good, Darin could pretend to be more interested in the Taj Zabbar war and in his family business than in her. He could stop mooning over her and treat her in a rude and perhaps even crude manner. He searched his mind for an example—and came up with his father's attitude toward women.

Darin wasn't sure he could even playact such arrogance. But he could try.

"You were lucky," he said in as cold a voice as he could remember his father using. He dropped her hand and slid a short distance away. "But foolish. Next time do as I tell you."

Her head came up and she glared at him. The exact reaction he had hoped she would have.

"Don't give me that." She folded her arms around her waist, as though he had delivered a blow. "You're alive because I brought you the gun. Just say thanks and be grateful I didn't follow your *orders*."

She had slipped right back into the wrong attitude. He would have to keep trying. Opening his mouth to deliver the next hit, he froze in midthought when a knock sounded at their door. Both of them jumped up and stared at the back of the door as if the knock had been a hiss from a poisonous viper.

"What'll we do?" she whispered.

He reached out toward the handle. "We'll answer and find out who it is."

When he opened the door, the porter was on the other side and a small commotion could be heard going on down the corridor. "*Pardon.* May I speak to monsieur and mademoiselle for a moment?"

"Certainly." Darin brought the man inside the cabin, but he stuck his head out past the threshold, trying to find out what was happening.

He turned around, shutting the door behind him. "What's going on?" he asked the porter.

"Ah, yes. The reason why I must speak with you. It is feared a terrible accident has occurred."

"An accident? What kind of accident?"

"A man has reportedly fallen off the train to his death."

Darin's blood pressure blew off the charts, but he forced a mild, surprised look instead of the guilt he was feeling. "Oh? What makes anyone think that?"

The porter lowered his voice conspiratorially. "A couple, older I believe, say they saw ze man fall. They were standing in a darkened compartment, staring out ze window, when zis form of a body passed by their view."

"Really? That seems odd. Are they sure?" Darin lowered his voice to match the other man's.

The porter nodded. "*Sì.* They say they were awakened by sounds—" he pointed above his head "—on ze roof. When they looked out...*le voilà!*"

Darin shot Rylie a look. She was pale, and he imagined he saw her trembling, but she pursed her lips and held herself together.

"What's happening now?" Darin asked the porter.

"The train staff, we are checking each compartment. We match tickets to passengers." He shook his head and rolled his eyes as if to say he did not believe their search would find anything. "If a man is missing, we will find out."

"Then what?" Rylie's voice was shaky, but Darin could hear her trying to stay strong.

"We arrive at ze town of Bellinzona momentarily. Ze Swiss police, they will question all passengers."

Darin's mind rifled through ideas. He couldn't speak to the police. He was no good at lying. Not like Tarik was.

When nothing else came to mind, he said, "Oh. But we were counting on resting at Bellinzona. And seeing the sights. My—" he gestured to Rylie "—my friend is not feeling too well. A little motion sickness, I think. Can't you help us out?"

While the man hesitated, Darin could feel the train slowing. Heard the slight screech of brakes against the rails. It was now or never.

Darin put his hand in his pocket and withdrew a wad of francs. He began peeling off bills, one at a time, and handing them over.

"*Sì,*" the man said as he shot a fast look at the closed

door behind him. "You are already checked by me, no? When ze train stops, I will lower steps from zis car for easy exit. You will go to the inn of my cousin. Unfortunately, not many hotels are to be found in Bellinzona. But La Villa di Ticino will be comfortable for the mademoiselle. Yes?"

Rylie put out her hand and gently touched the man's arm. "Thank you."

The porter bowed his head, his eyes twinkling with concern for her in return. *"Sì. Sì."* He patted her hand. "The train, it will stop for several hours, mademoiselle. You may rest easy at the villa."

Maybe Rylie would rest easy. But Darin wouldn't rest at all until she was on her way out of the country, out of Europe and away from both the danger—and from him.

Fifty miles away in Milan, Sheikh Newaf Bin Hamad Taj Zabbar prepared for a mourning ritual by donning the ceremonial white tunic and red sash. The colors of innocence and blood.

In his mind he chanted the ancient rituals. Rituals based on the unique mysticism of a historical militant sect. These teachings, brought from across the centuries via the god of Time, were given to Taj Zabbar elders by their tutors and guardians—the early Assassins.

Their one true belief, the foremost revelation by the Sheik of the Mountain, was clear to everyone who followed. *All that matters is action.* Action, along with total loyalty to the master.

According to the teachings, a loyal warrior's suicide and martyrdom shall lead to the Assassins' paradise in the Shadow of Swords. But Hamad had read the historical facts and knew that the original sect of Assassins, called the Nizari, had built a model paradise in a valley near Persia. They had wished to fool their followers into devoting their lives and deaths to the sect.

The Assassins' very real paradise on earth was described in detail centuries ago by the great Marco Polo after he was brought to the valley by the original Imams.

> In a beautiful valley...lies a luxurious garden stored with every delicious fruit and every fragrant shrub.... Palaces of various sizes are to be found, ornamented with works of gold, with paintings and with furniture of rich silks. By means of small conduits...streams of wine, milk, honey and some of pure water were seen to flow in every direction.... Elegant and beautiful damsels, accomplished in the arts of singing, playing upon all sorts of musical instruments, dancing, and especially those of dalliance and amorous allurement were seen continually sporting and amusing themselves in the garden....

Such a description of paradise might be enough to lure some into martyrdom, but Hamad preferred to find his own paradise in life first. He vowed to maintain at least one of the teachings of his ancestors: *death and blood shall bring followers the reward of eternal life.* As part of that doctrine, Hamad would use the mourning ritual to assist his foolish cousin Taweel forward to his death's reward.

Hamad could've predicted such an end to his not-terribly-bright employee. The man was not a snake, as his ancestors demanded of their followers. Nor was he fit to wield the poisonous dagger.

The Taj Zabbar were descended from the best of the Assassins. And Hamad believed he was the best of the best. Deadly—of course. But smart, too. Smart enough to use modern means to rid himself of both enemies and unworthy friends. He had been informed of the exact instant when his cousin's life had expired. The computer chip implanted in his chest had showed the time of death with an immediate transmission to Hamad's computers. A great cheer had gone up among the men at Taweel's martyrdom.

"Pardon the interruption, my sheik." Another of Hamad's men entered his private chamber after a quick knock. "You asked to be informed about the progress of the train. It has stopped at Bellinzona and will be searched by the Swiss police."

"And the whereabouts of the coded communiqué sent by the elder Mugrin?" Hamad was still annoyed over the elder's stupid and dangerous choice of writing his message down on paper. Certainly, that elder would have to be eliminated sooner rather than later after this move.

"It is believed the Kadir son known as Darin still has it in his possession, my sheik."

"And do we also believe the Hunt woman continues to travel with Darin Kadir?"

"Yes, Excellency."

This news might be good. Hamad could bring down several threats with one throw of his dagger.

"I want a team of our best trained men—men trained in the ways of our ancestors. Send them to the train and waste no time bringing the communiqué back to me."

"What about the woman?"

It took a few seconds for Hamad to make a decision about the woman. "If it is possible, bring the woman alive, as well. We have profitable uses for a beautiful woman such as that one."

"And if it is not possible?"

Fuming over too many questions about a subject that should be clear, Hamad narrowed his eyes at his assistant. "It is the communiqué that is all-important. It must not be allowed to be decoded by the Kadirs. Do whatever you think necessary to bring it to me. I don't really care what you do with either the man or the woman to accomplish this task. The Taj Zabbar war of retribution has been uncovered. The Kadirs now know the truth. There is no need for further secrecy."

"Yes, my sheik." The man backed out of the room and quietly shut the door.

Hamad bowed to the makeshift altar before him. Gingerly picking up the ceremonial dagger, he used the blade to slice a line across his wrist. Bloodred droplets spattered onto the stark-white linen cloth.

A Taj Zabbar warrior must be honored and assisted to his paradise. Revenge for his death would be had later— all in due time. Hamad recited the seven mystical laws based on personal concentration and supreme loyalty, clearing the way for cousin Taweel to his paradise.

"Enjoy your reward for the effort you expended, my cousin." Hamad whispered the chants against the roar of time moving forward and then added a personal postscript. "Darin Kadir shall join you on your journey, cousin, before the sun sets over Zabbaran once more. I swear to it."

"Come on." Rylie swung back around, urging Darin to follow her down the train tracks and into the old town of Bellinzona. "What's wrong with you? I thought you were the one who wanted to sneak away from the train until the cops were finished questioning people."

Darin stood, staring at something on the outside of the car they had exited—but finally he turned. "Huh? Oh, yes. Let's go."

He was certainly acting strange. Almost as if he were trying to memorize which car they'd left. But why?

She grabbed hold of his shirtsleeve and dragged him along beside her. When they rounded the end car of the train, they had to make a dash for the dark shelter of an alley between the edge of the station and the old rock buildings beyond.

La Villa di Ticino was six long blocks away. Rylie wouldn't feel really safe until they made it there.

Considering all the commotion at the train station, the town itself seemed fairly quiet. A few street vendors were selling their wares along the sidewalks closest to the station. But at dawn, not many other people seemed to be out and about.

"Hold on a minute." Darin dragged his feet, tugged against her hand and brought her back toward him.

He pointed to a large black shawl hanging over a street vendor's wagon. Within seconds Darin had negotiated a price with the vendor and was draping the handmade treasure around her head and body. It almost covered her completely from head to toe in black knit. And after being put into place, the shawl left her practically suffocating and nearly blind.

"That should help keep us from being discovered while we travel these streets," Darin told her as he threw his arm around her shoulders and helped her navigate the cobblestone walks.

"You think we look like a local couple now?"

"Not to the locals. But hopefully to the national police, at least from a distance."

Rylie shifted enough inside the shawl so that she could see out. They raced past five-hundred-year-old castles and a few even older churches that had been made entirely out of rough-cut stone. She worked hard not to trip on the uneven terrain.

The medieval architecture and the quiet morning should've been enough to bring her peace—and maybe would some other time. But right this moment her heart was pounding and her palms sweating as they hurried along toward the inn.

At last they came to the side street where La Villa di Ticino was located. A small sign swinging over an old wooden door was the only marker. As she was about to knock, the door opened.

"Buon giorno! Vieni dentro." A stout, middle-aged woman beamed at them as she dragged them over the threshold and into a small reception area.

"Did you know we were coming?"

"Sì. The nephew of my husband…the porter from your train…he calls to say you need refuge. *Benvenuti al nostro albergo.* Welcome to our inn."

"Thanks," Darin said gruffly as he slid a protective arm around Rylie's waist and moved in closer. "Can you just show us to a room, please?"

Rylie knew exactly what he was feeling. This woman seemed too friendly. Too outgoing. Too glad to see them.

Relieved when they were finally alone and locked inside a Spartan room, Rylie collapsed on the one queen-size bed. "I didn't think we would make it."

"I didn't, either. But I'm not sure I like the feel of this place. Something in my gut says it's not right."

She nodded. "Yeah. Have you checked the windows?"

Darin made a quick trip around the room to assess where they had found themselves. Then he went into the bathroom, came back and closed and locked windows, knocked on walls and looked behind the two paintings on display. Finally he spent a little time in the closet, checking out the walls in there in case of any false doors.

"Actually, this place is made like a fortress," he said when he was back beside her. "The walls are thick. I'm guessing several feet thick and made from solid stone. See there?" He pointed to the wires dangling from the ceiling. "They've had to string cords around the room in order to bring in electricity and modernize the place. The two windows in here have interior wood shutters that I've shut and locked. We're closed up enough now that we could be in a cave—or a fortress."

Darin was the one who was closed up. They had to stay put for the next few hours, and if he kept this nervous tension up he could have a meltdown or a heart attack by the time it was safe to leave. He had taken on the entire responsibility for keeping them from harm, and it wasn't fair. Rylie wanted to say something, do something that would help him relax.

"We've managed to get rather filthy in the last couple of days, don't you think?" She took a few steps toward the bathroom. "How're the facilities? Can we catch a couple of quick showers while we wait for the police to finish?"

Darin stared at her as though she'd lost her mind.

"Yeah, I know our lives are at stake. Believe me, I know. But we're stuck here for the next few hours at least. What else can we do? Besides, I feel sticky."

She stuck her head in the small room off the bedroom. A tiny sink with an even tinier mirror above it hung at an awkward angle against one wall. A small claw-footed tub had been squeezed against the other wall. And a miniature toilet with hardly enough room to sit down was wedged into a corner and was the only other thing in the small space.

She'd hoped for an oversize tub made for two. But no such luck. Well, she wasn't sure she could've talked Darin into the tub with her anyway. Though after the two of them were cleaned up, she fully intended to wrangle him into that nice big bed. This was as good a time as any to test her theory about the tension between them dissolving as soon as their raging lust was satiated.

"We could talk." Darin gazed at her with a sober, bruised look. Those dark-as-midnight eyes still held in deep, dark secrets.

"You mean *you* could talk and I could listen? No thanks. Not while we both stink. The showers come first."

And after that—the sex. Talking could wait.

"Go right ahead and hop in," he told her. "I want to call my brother. And maybe I'll speak to the innkeeper about breakfast while I'm at it. Are you hungry?"

Not for food. "Coffee and a roll might be nice."

"Okay, I'll take care of it. Don't rush. I'll clean up, myself, after you're done."

Yes, you will, Darin Kadir, she thought. *Today is the day when we'll clean up our lives, both physically and emotionally. We'll push away all the secrets so at last we can figure out where we stand.*

You can count on that.

Chapter 10

"No need to drive to Bellinzona," Darin assured his brother over the phone. "We've met a train porter who will be sure we reach the Milan station safely."

"Of course he will." Tarik's skepticism came through in his voice, even over the sound of running water as Rylie took her shower not ten feet away. "You will hand over the coded document the minute you reach the Milan station. Right? One of our men will fly it and Rylie to headquarters." Tarik didn't sound too crazy about the idea, but it was a plan.

"I'd prefer it if you would use one of our own jets to fly Rylie home to Texas. And make her as comfortable as possible."

"You're sure she'll be willing to leave?" Tarik's tone mocked him. "Shakir tells me she seemed pretty determined to stay until she has all the facts concerning that explosion in Houston."

Darin lowered his voice, though he was positive no one could hear him. "She already knows the Taj Zabbar were responsible. And I intend to make sure she's ready to go by the time we reach Milan. Leave her to me."

Tarik's low chuckle was loud enough to be heard even through his sat phone. "Yeah, and you've always been so great at convincing the ladies to do anything. Listen, maybe I should..."

"No thanks, baby brother." Darin worked to release his tight jaw as he reached over for his coffee cup. "You take care of getting your men ready for an assault on that Milan address I found. I'll be in time to join you at the takedown. I want to be there when we learn what they're planning—and their identities. Wait for me to arrive before you move in, will you?"

"As you wish. You deserve to be in on this first skirmish, Darin. But I won't be a bit surprised if your lady friend shows up there, too. Make sure she stays out of our way."

It was all Darin could do not to hurl his cup at a wall. "Shut up, bro. You do your job and I'll see to it she makes it on that plane."

Without waiting for another snide remark, Darin closed his phone and set it on the bedside table. Except for that annoying conversation with his brother, Darin was feeling a lot more relaxed about being stuck at this inn for the next few hours. The signora had delivered up strong coffee and fresh pastries without any complaints. She'd brought warm bath towels and a replacement travel kit, containing shampoo, toothpaste, a brush and razor, to replace the one Rylie was using in the bathroom.

Cheerful, much like her cousin the porter, the innkeeper had even volunteered to launder their clothes while they caught a couple hours of sleep.

She'd come by to collect Rylie's things along with his pullover shirt and zip-up jacket, leaving him naked to the waist. But he'd decided Rylie had been right. It would be a real pleasure to arrive in Milan clean and pressed.

While he'd waited for Rylie to finish in the shower, Darin had come up with another plan to get rid of her. As smart as she was, the woman seemed to have some kind of death wish. And he would be damned if Rylie was going to kill herself while he was standing nearby.

This time around, he'd decided the plan needed to use friendship and loyalty as a hook for pleading his case with her about doing the right thing. She was certain to understand what was honorable. He knew they at least had that much in common. In fact, Darin himself felt somewhat desperate, for once in his life, to do the right thing by a woman he cared about.

Sure that he understood Rylie rather well by this point in their relationship, Darin knew she would value friendship above any small matters of pride. And that was but one way they were alike in their thinking.

He thought back to what she'd done in the name of honor, for instance. Maybe she'd gone about it wrong, but Rylie had been trying to honor her family's name by selling off their assets and taking care of the victims of the explosion. Darin was also empathetic to her compulsion to honor her father's memory by proving that Red Hunt had not been the cause of the explosion. Rylie now understood that truth the same way that Darin knew the truth of the Taj Zabbar's covert war against his family.

Yes, the two of them had similar views and opinions on several subjects. This was no small matter in the big scheme of things. They shared views about right and honor and putting family first. Her safety seemed to be their one big sticking point.

The bathroom door opened and Rylie stepped into the bedroom, halfway disappearing in the cloud of steam that accompanied her. Darin nearly swallowed his tongue. Her hair was wrapped in one towel and her body was wrapped in another. He knew she didn't have on a single thing underneath.

Waiting a beat for his pulse to settle, he pointed at the coffee and rolls because he couldn't utter a word.

"Where are all my clothes?"

He cleared his throat. "The signora is laundering them. She just brought in the coffee."

"I don't even have any underwear to put on?"

Shaking his head, he tried for a look of chagrin. But he couldn't pretend to be overwrought about her problem. Not when his veins were sizzling and his libido was taking too much notice.

Rylie gave him a most unusual glance. He had a feeling she was thinking of something else, something he should've been able to figure out. But he was having trouble thinking at all. His brain had fogged over at the first sight of her.

It was time to back away while he still could. "My turn in the shower?"

"Yes. But hurry back."

He made a hasty retreat and eased the door shut

behind him. How had he gotten himself into this situation?

Could he still do the right thing? Silently laughing at his own sudden uncertainty, Darin discovered he could barely even speak, let alone convince her to leave for her own safety and his piece of mind.

But he wasn't some randy teenager stunned by his first sight of a naked woman. He was thirty-two, the vice CEO of a multinational business, and experienced in the sensual ways of womankind. Furthermore, he was strong-willed—and strong-minded. He could do anything if he concentrated hard enough.

Gathering his wits and promising to banish erotic thoughts and any hesitation, he stepped into the shower and flipped the water all the way to cold. Maybe if he stayed in here long enough, he could convince himself that even while talking to the naked woman in the next room he could still manage to do the right thing.

When the water from the faucet slowed to a trickle, Darin quickly shaved and dried off. After stepping back into his slacks, he stood with his hand on the doorknob, building up his nerve to face her again.

Taking a deep breath, he threw open the door with a flourish. While striding into the room like he knew what he was doing, Darin tried to think up some clever way to begin their conversation.

But he stopped midstride, astonished to find her sprawled across the bed with the black shawl covering all her important parts. Asleep.

He'd known she was exhausted. They hadn't had any restful sleep in over thirty-six hours. But he had been all set for their talk. Grateful for a reprieve, he glanced down at her face. So peaceful and beautiful. She needed sleep more than she needed a conversation about hard truths. Perhaps he would be better off to slip on his shoes and go have a nice long, boring conversation with the innkeeper instead.

Good idea. Still, Darin couldn't take his eyes off the figure in the bed. Noticing that her shawl had slipped, revealing the swell of one creamy breast, he leaned over to push it back in place. But when his fingers touched the warmth of her skin, she opened her eyes.

"Hi," she murmured with a lazy drawl. "All done in the shower?"

"Mmm." He coughed and then added, "Go back to sleep. I thought I'd go visiting, maybe make another telephone call."

She reached out to him. "Stay. Come lie down with me."

What his body urged him to do at that moment was as far from the right thing as he could imagine. "You don't want this, Rylie."

He sat at the very edge of the bed when she said nothing. "I've been thinking about your future. A lot. My family is about to embark on what has the potential to be a long, drawn-out mission. A mission fraught with danger at every turn. You, on the other hand, must go back to Texas and honor your family and their business. They need you to make things right."

"Darin…"

He shook his head. "Just listen. You and I have found each other despite the most outrageous of circumstances. I'd like to think that in only a few days we've formed a bond…a friendship that can last a lifetime. But if we do this—"

It was all he could do not to beg to do exactly what she was suggesting.

Straightening his shoulders, he took her hand. "We can't. It could ruin everything between us."

She shook her head. "Not *everything*. Don't you trust me? I trust you."

"If you mean, do I trust that you have no illnesses and have taken care of yourself—of course I do. You may trust me on that account, too. But becoming intimate too soon destroys relationships. I don't want that to happen to you and me. We shouldn't."

Rylie sat up, ignoring the shawl as it slid down to her waist. "We should. And maybe it will ruin things, or maybe it will provide us some interesting answers instead."

Darin was dying a thousand deaths, wishing he could simply take her in his arms. The sight of her naked to the waist had left him panting.

"You…you're so beautiful, Rylie. And I *do* want you, but…"

"What *I* want—" she pulled herself up on her knees, the shawl pooling on the bed, and then reached out to him "—is for you to touch me…hold me…make me forget about families and wars and death. Make love to me, Darin. Now. We only have a little while."

That did it. He surrendered. Darin could never turn away from her while she begged, even if it was the right thing to do.

When he touched her—when he drew her into his arms—it felt less like a surrender and more like an awakening. This was good—right. Being here with this strong woman, who clearly wanted him, was turning into exactly what *he* needed to make things right.

Darin had never been with a woman before who wanted him quite as much. Nor with one who could turn him into a quivering mass of expectation as Rylie had done. Something about this whole spur-of-the-moment thing suddenly felt big—huge.

He experienced a moment of pure panic. Then Rylie leaned in close and kissed him.

Whispering against his mouth, she said, "You have too much on." She rubbed her breasts against his bare chest, creating the most exquisite friction, while she reached for his zipper.

"Careful. Things are already tight down there, and becoming more dangerous by the moment." He stood, disposing of the slacks himself.

The look on her face as he stood before her in all his glory was priceless. He would never forget it.

Her skin was flushed. Her eyes glazed. The budded tips of her breasts jutted up toward him. Smiling, she carefully took his erection in both her hands, gently caressing his swollen flesh. He couldn't move—could barely speak.

She bent her head, but halted at the last moment and gazed up at him.

His knees buckled and he sucked in air. "Rylie," he gasped. "Wait."

She let her eyes do all the smiling as she flicked her tongue over his sensitive tip. "I'm done waiting."

Lowering her chin, she closed in enough to plant a baby-soft kiss against the part of him pulsing in expectation. He called out her name—and then promptly forgot his own.

Rylie was on her knees before him in a submissive position, but she wasn't fooled. Pleased with herself, she knew she held all the power. She took him hard into her mouth.

All the power. The idea was an aphrodisiac, spurring her on as he dug his fingers though her hair and moaned. His pleasure became her pleasure. She took him higher, closer to an edge, then backed away. Tasting. Licking. Controlling.

The more he trusted her to set the pace, the more intense was her gratification. She heard her own moans coming from someplace deep within her throat as they ramped up the friction. Wrapping her arms around his hips, she captured him in the most intimate of embraces. The idea of a total possession, in both body and mind, flicked across her consciousness…right before she fully gave up to the insanity.

Crazed with dizzying power and need, as soon as Darin drew back she went with him and collapsed in a heap on the bed. But she cautioned herself to hold off. For one heartbeat she waited, intent on finding out if he would insist on controlling their new positions. To her amazement, he rolled on his back and pulled her up his body, inviting her to decide where to go from here—and giving her the freedom to do as she wanted.

And she wanted. Oh, how she wanted.

Straddling his hips, she pressed her palms to his shoulders and grinned down at him. "Gotcha. Right where I want you. You are my prisoner."

"Do with me what you will," he teased, but in a dazed voice. "I am at your command."

Absolutely positive that there had never been a better sexual fantasy in the history of the world, Rylie leaned over and offered her breasts by brushing them across his lips. He licked and stroked each until he finally lifted his head off the bed enough to fully capture one in his mouth.

Even though she was on top, it soon became a question of who was tempting whom. Drawing the sensitive tip into his mouth with a greedy gulp, he alternately sucked and soothed. Tormenting her until she issued a sensual moan from somewhere deep inside her, he nipped at each nipple. And with each small pain came a resulting electric shock of pleasure.

Wet and slick, and so hungry to feel him inside her that she was wild with the desire for it, she lifted her hips and positioned herself over the head of his erection. Darin put his hands at the sides of her hips to help guide her, and she felt his whole body tense with anticipation.

Her heart pounded. Her muscles tightened along with his.

She had never been so sure of anything in her whole life.

Unbelievable heat. Wet. Hot. Tight.

As Rylie slowly lowered her body down to cover him, Darin's last coherent thought was again of surrender. He had thought he'd given himself over to her hands. Yet now they were both giving and taking and rejoicing in each other's needs. Neither one had given in. Both had succumbed.

Gripping her hips as she lifted her bottom, he helped her rise up, inch by incredible inch. He waited, holding his breath until she hesitated at the very tip, and then he rammed his hips up at the same time as she brought hers down with a hard slam.

His breath exploded from his lungs on a sharp rush.

Her breathing became labored as he continued guiding her up and down. Between one lungful of air and the next, they began moving as one. The pressure built. The pace increased.

They worked together in a frenzied motion that belied how he felt. He wanted this to last forever, yet he was racing toward the finish line. It was too much. It was not nearly enough.

He gazed up at her, watching as her chest rose and fell. Watching as she fought her release. He couldn't help himself. He pinched her nipples between thumb and forefinger. Once. Twice. Her eyes opened wide in her pleasure.

"Keep your eyes open," he begged her. "Look at me."

Higher and higher they climbed toward the peak. But she did as he asked and locked onto his gaze.

In one of the most erotic moments of his entire life, he watched her eyes as he reached down between them and rubbed a thumb against her sensitive nub. He felt the electric shock as it careened through her body. Her eyes rolled back in her head.

She finally gave in to it and came on a long, delicious shudder. Her internal muscles sucked and milked at him like a dangerous undertow. The sheer power of it brought him to his own release.

Too soon the astounding sensations totally consumed and inflamed him with majesty and euphoria. The enormous explosion of heat and fire seemed to go on and on.

He rolled with it, let it arc over them both. She collapsed against his chest, melted and boneless. Both of them gasped for air, hearts pounding and sweat pouring. His arms cocooned her against the outside world as he let her fall asleep in that position.

There would be no sleep for him. It took a moment for his head to clear. But when it did, thoughts zinged around his brain.

This woman was his. Had to be his.

Embarrassing emotions he had ducked his entire life leaked out of his heart right along with the tears leaking quietly from his eyes. When she shifted in his arms and breathed against his chest, he knew his obsession was going to be a lifetime curse.

How had this happened? He'd never wanted anyone to become this important. This necessary to his very existence.

The last time anyone had meant this much, she'd died. His mother had died. And he had failed her.

Darin knew he'd failed her because his father had always acted as though he believed it to be true. Believed that his sons had contributed to their mother's demise. Crazy or not, Darin had done everything he could to make up for it. To prove he was strong and smart—and worthy of a father's love.

Now here was yet another person whom he felt he should prove something to. Whom he could not fail. Darin's only mission in life from now on was to protect Rylie. Keep her from any harm. It was no longer a choice but a command that came from somewhere so deeply buried that he would never admit that he recognized it for what it truly was.

Love.

Looking down at her peaceful face and her thick

auburn lashes lying quietly against her cheek, Darin knew only one thing. Felt the certainty of only one thing.

Mine to cherish, he thought. *Mine* to always protect.

Chapter 11

Rylie woke up groggy and disoriented. She'd just had the sexiest dream imaginable.

Trying to roll over, she found herself entangled in broad, buff arms and pinned down by heavy, muscular thighs. Darin. Not a dream at all, but the most sensual experience of her entire life. Without thinking, she almost turned into him, ready to show him how much what they'd shared had mattered to her.

Damn it. She froze, her mind reeling over exactly how much being with Darin *had* really mattered. Now what was she supposed to do?

She'd been counting on having so-so sex with the man. Instead, he'd turned her whole theory about them being incompatible on its head. She had pushed him and teased him, sure he would never give her the mutual respect she knew she must have.

And what did he do? He gave her magic.

Damn it. She'd seen a whole new side to Darin, and it scared the hell out of her.

Torn now, with one part of her wanting to wake him up with kisses and declaring her undying love. And the other part of her wanting to sneak out of the room without waking him so she could run like hell. Rylie was on the verge of becoming unglued.

Damn it. And damn him for making her want to believe in happily-ever-afters for the first time in her life.

How crazy must she be? Crazy enough to be stupid, that's what. They'd known each other for a grand total of what? Three whole days? Lifetime commitments didn't come in such neat little packages. Her parents had known each other for most of their lives when they'd finally gotten married. Her mother said it took that long to develop respect and deep regard for another's feelings. Besides, every quickie overnight affair Rylie had ever heard of had ended sooner rather than later. And had ended badly to boot.

Yet all of her knowledge, all of her warnings to herself, meant exactly nothing when she thought about how he'd gazed into her eyes. With looks that seemed to say he wanted her to be his Cinderella. The more she thought about it, the more she went into panic mode. She'd been playing at some kind of crazy, stupid game and now it looked like she would get burned as a booby prize.

Trying to quiet her traitorous pounding heart, Rylie searched her mind for sensible reasons for why she should be feeling this way about him. Was it simply a matter of an adrenaline letdown? She'd read about how people who had been in life-and-death situations sometimes needed to have a sexual encounter in order to prove to themselves that they were really alive.

That might be true in some cases, but it was not applicable here. Surely they were safe. At least for a while. Furthermore, it had been all her idea long before they'd done that scary top-of-the-train balancing act.

Well, dang. Where did any of that leave her?

Falling in love?

But she didn't want that. Could. Not. Have. That. Not with a man whose family took part in international espionage and covert wars of retribution with centuries-old enemies. It was crazy—stupid!

Again she asked the question: *Where did that leave her?*

The answer came into her head loud and clear. It left her running for her life. As soon as she could get dressed and find her way back to Geneva.

She tried to slide out from under his arm, but Darin only tightened his grip around her.

"Hi," he said in a rough voice. "I don't guess we have enough time for a repeat performance?"

She twisted out of his embrace and sat up, dragging the shawl around her chest as she went. "No way. In fact, I'm beginning to worry about our clothes being ready in time for us to catch the train. Can you check on them while I clean up a little?"

She wasn't going to talk to him about splitting up at the train station and each going their own way. Not yet. One glance at Darin told her he was already staring at her like she'd slapped him.

Not ready to face any after-the-fact discussions, Rylie scurried from the bed, still trailing the shawl. How could she talk to him about something when she hadn't even settled it in her own mind yet? She took two steps toward the bathroom before he spoke.

"Aren't we...can't we talk first?"

She refused to turn around. "Talk about what? Everything's all set, right? I mean with your brothers and the Taj Zabbar."

"Yes, that part is all set. That's not what I want to talk about."

"Oh?" She bounced on her toes, ready to make a mad dash into the bathroom. "What did you want to say?"

"I wanted to talk about what just happened to us in this bed." Now his voice was sounding all edgy and pissy.

Well, too bad. She did not have time for either recriminations or regrets. "Um... It was great. Really. Best sex ever. But you know we can't take a chance of missing that train. Please go check on our clothes."

"Great sex?" The sound of his voice was...hurt...and it made her finally turn around.

"Darin, I don't know what you want from me. It was really, *really* terrific sex. But we can't be late."

He turned away from her to step into his slacks, though first she'd seen the most heart-wrenching look pass over his face. What had he wanted her to say? Obviously something she hadn't given him. Now Rylie was totally confused. She certainly hadn't meant to hurt him.

"Get ready," he told her as he opened the door to the hall. "I'll get our clothes from the innkeeper. Be back in a minute."

Twenty minutes later, Rylie still felt a little crazy-stupid. Neither she nor Darin had spoken one word since he'd left to pick up their clothes. But at this point, the two of them were dressed and nearly ready to leave for the station.

Darin was pocketing his things. He'd stored his weapon, passport, phone and cash in the nightstand's drawer alongside her waist purse. A casual thought occurred to her out of the blue. Where was the leather portfolio that he'd been carrying? She hadn't seen anything of it since before they'd gotten on the train. Had he left it in Geneva? She thought about asking, but it was time to go.

Darin seemed satisfied that everything was stashed and after giving the room one last going over, he turned to her. "Ready?"

His eyes were still brooding, sad. Rylie couldn't manage to say a word for fear she would break down entirely and spill words that she hadn't had the time to consider.

She nodded. He turned the doorknob and stood aside to let her go first.

Stepping across the threshold, Rylie felt as if she were leaving behind a special place. And a special time. For one second she wished they could go backward for a few hours. She turned to give the room one last glance and caught Darin's gaze.

He was watching her closely, and it seemed to her that he was blinking back a sheen of wetness. She opened her mouth to say something, anything, when all of a sudden his gaze flicked away to glance at something over her shoulder. Before she could judge whether this new look was one of anger or terror, she was roughly grabbed from behind and shoved hard.

Darin reached for the gun at his back, but a deeply

accented voice came from right behind her. "Don't try it, Kadir. Not if you want her to live."

A strong arm, clothed in rough cloth, came around her throat. Immediately she was pulled up tightly against the solid wall of the man's chest. A man whom she had yet to see.

Darin took a step forward. "Don't hurt her."

Rylie felt the sharp edge of a knife blade digging into her throat. She squeaked when the blade broke her skin.

Darin raised his hands, offered up his weapon and stepped back. "Okay. Okay. Stop! I'll do whatever you say."

The shadow of a man dressed in Middle Eastern–style robes brushed past her and disarmed Darin. After pocketing the gun, the fellow casually slammed his fist into Darin's face. Hard. Darin's body stumbled backward and hit the wall beside the bed.

Rylie could do nothing but whimper.

Then a third man, a great bear of a guy, stepped around the man who was holding on to her. This third, huge man had his fist wrapped around the throat of a much smaller man, and he was dragging the poor little fellow beside him.

Rylie was stunned to realize the smaller man was their porter from the train. Blood trickled from the porter's ear and he was crying.

Instead of feeling panic, Rylie became angry at such injustice and furious over the treatment they and the porter were receiving from these thugs. But she was in no position to help. So she silently swore to get even as soon as she could get the chance.

The Middle Easterner grabbed the front of Darin's

shirt and pulled him forward to spit in his face. "You have property that does not belong to you, Kadir dog," he snarled.

Darin started to shake his head, but he never got the chance. The big bear of a guy dropped the half-conscious porter in a heap on the floor like a rag doll. Then he reached out and raised Darin off his feet, using only a two-fisted grip. Slamming Darin down hard again, bear-guy held on to him with one enormous hand while ripping Darin's jacket right off his body with the other. As Darin's arms were yanked from his sleeves, Rylie swore she could hear popping sounds as if his shoulders were being pulled from their sockets.

Darin winced and tried to fight, but bear-guy backhanded him and rocked a fist into his gut with such force she was surprised when it didn't rip his body in half.

Oh, Darin.

Rylie tried to inch out of the hold she was caught up in, but with her first move, the man behind her tightened his grip and pushed the blade farther into her skin. She felt blood leaking down her neck and realized she had no choice but to stay quiet and watch as Darin was stripped, frisked and beaten.

When he lay moaning on the floor, minus all clothing except for his slacks, the Middle Eastern–looking man turned to her. "Are you carrying our property, whore?"

She was afraid to speak. Couldn't even move enough to shake her head.

Everything was mostly a blur after that. She remembered the big man moving into her space and roughly patting down her body. When he felt her travel purse, bear-guy stopped, and in a move so swift it shocked her stupid, he tore the T-shirt up and over her head. Standing there with only her bra for cover from the waist up, she began to shake. The next thing Rylie saw coming at her was the tip of a sharp, slender knife.

In the background, she heard Darin calling out for them to stop, but the knife's arc never halted. She cried out, sure she was about to die. With one long downward slice, bear-guy cut the purse right off her body, leaving an angry-looking gash down her rib cage.

Too hysterical to cry, Rylie bent over and grabbed her shirt from the floor while bear-guy stayed busy demolishing her purse and tearing into her passport and cell phone. Next thing she knew, the Middle Eastern–looking man nodded at bear guy. Rylie was afraid of what came next.

The bigger man proceeded to tear the room apart, using both the knife and his bare hands. He ripped the mattress to shreds. The nightstand was turned over and smashed to bits. It occurred to her that all this commotion should bring the innkeeper—or the police. But all remained silent.

Trembling, but not being held at knifepoint at the moment, Rylie slipped on her shirt again and went to kneel at Darin's side.

"How badly are you hurt?" she whispered.

He turned his head and tried to wink at her out of an eye already swollen and blue. "I'm okay. Stay alive, Rylie. No matter what else happens. You stay alive."

"I will, Darin, I promise…."

At that moment, the big man stopped tearing up the room, reached down and yanked Darin to his feet. Darin swayed but stayed upright.

"Once more, Kadir," the Middle Eastern man began.

"Where is our property?" Then he turned and grabbed Rylie by the hair, jerking her up beside him.

He placed a long-barrelled gun to her temple. "Quick. Tell me or she is dead."

"It's on the train. I swear I left it in our sleeping car."

The Middle Eastern man exploded in a voice at once low yet loud in his throat. "Liar! We checked that car."

Silently, bear-guy put his big, meaty hands around Darin's throat and began to squeeze. Darin tried to fight him off, but the other man was at least twice his size.

Rylie closed her eyes so she couldn't see down the barrel of the gun and held her breath, waiting for her end to come. *I'm sorry, Darin. I tried to stay alive.*

She expected to hear the last click and explosion she would ever hear coming from a gun before it was all over and everything went black. Instead, Rylie could hardly believe what she heard. The Middle Eastern man began speaking a few soft words to his comrades in an odd language. Her eyes popped open and she saw bear-guy drop a still-breathing Darin like a hot rock. The Middle Eastern–looking guy, apparently the boss, was now holding a phone to his ear and not a gun to her head.

Ohmygod. Both she and Darin were still alive. And if she could stay alive like she'd promised him, there was always a chance of clocking these dudes. Of showing them a little Texas justice.

Rylie bit down on her tongue to keep her mouth shut and bided her time until she could make a move against them. And oh man, she couldn't wait.

* * *

Hamad Taj Zabbar was seething as his hired man tried to explain the situation over the phone. "The communiqué!" he shouted into the speaker. "We must have it."

"We have searched both the train car and the entire villa, master. And we have searched the persons of the man and woman. The communiqué is not to be found."

Never trust a subordinate to do what you should do yourself. "Is the man still alive? What has he told you?"

"Yes, he is alive. The Kadir dog swore he left the papers on the train. But we searched. It is not so."

Hamad hesitated over his next move, wishing he knew more about this particular Kadir brother.

His assassin-trained employee spoke up out of turn. "Shall we kill them both, my sheik?"

"No, you fool. Kadir is the only one who knows where he put the papers." Hamad quickly sifted through what little he knew of Darin Kadir. "You found the man and woman together in a room at the villa. Is that right?"

"This is true."

Then without question, Hamad knew what he must do. "Bring them both here to me. Keep them alive."

"Yes, master. Shall we eliminate their conspirators?"

"You mean the porter and the innkeeper? It is not necessary. Tie them and leave them. It is very possible we may yet need them alive."

Hamad felt certain the porter had no knowledge of the whereabouts of the communiqué. The man had fallen apart with only minor torture and quickly disclosed everything he'd known. Yet if the Hunt woman did not prove to be the impetus for obtaining the truth from Darin Kadir, then the porter's life might be worth using in trade.

"How long will it take to bring Kadir and the Hunt woman here to Milan?"

"We must drive, my sheik. The train left Bellinzona an hour ago."

"A couple of hours, then. Very well. Keep them both hidden, and hurry."

Tarik Kadir stood on a siding at the Milan train station, hands on his hips and questions burning in his brain. "And you are sure this is the sleeping car where my brother and the Hunt woman were passengers?"

"Yes, sir." One of Tarik's Italian investigators stood beside him in the warm sun as the two stared up at the uncoupled car. "The Swiss police gave it a quick once-over in Bellinzona during their search for the missing man.

"But somewhere between there and here," the investigator continued, "your brother's compartment was tossed. Cushions and mattresses were slashed and storage bins broken apart. The porter, your brother and his friend are missing. The Italian police have set the car aside here and mean to go over it again tomorrow for evidence."

"I need a few minutes inside first. Is that possible?"

"Yes, of course. Not a problem. The Italian police are your friends." The investigator casually waved a hand toward the car's steps, inviting Tarik aboard.

Tarik had been trying to reach Darin for the last

couple of hours with no luck. But he hadn't been overly concerned with his brother's lack of communication until his man called a while ago, announcing that Darin had failed to arrive at the Milan station. Tarik already had a couple of men on their way to Bellinzona, the last place Darin had made contact. But he had little hope of locating his older brother there.

As he took the steps up to the sleeping car, a memory of a young Darin, trying his best to console his two little brothers after their mother's death, crept into Tarik's mind. Without Darin, Tarik never would've made it to adulthood. He owed his oldest brother his life.

Damn Darin anyway. He had no business playing at being an investigator with a group as dangerous as the Taj Zabbar. Tarik's heart ached at the real possibility of losing his big brother.

But Tarik would not let that happen, despite the difficult circumstances. Their mission had already been complicated when his team surrounded the apartment where the Taj Zabbar leader was supposedly having a meeting, only to find the place empty.

Walking down the train corridor, Tarik headed for his brother's former compartment. It was worth a look.

After that, Tarik would make use of his nervous energy and do what he did best. Locate the bad guys— and then locate his brother.

Darin had better still be alive or there would be hell to pay. The Taj Zabbar thought they were at war now? Ha! They had no idea what a real war of retribution could look like.

Chapter 12

Rylie stared mournfully through the dirty piece of glass next to her head at the traffic driving by. Too bad it wasn't a true roll-down window but only a filthy, stationary sheet of glass. Not that she could've done much had it been a real window. Being hog-tied the way she was left little room for movement.

Sighing at the frustration of her situation, she let her head roll back on the cracked leather seat. Their three attackers took up most of the room in this old European car. Most of the air, too. She'd found herself squished into a tiny corner of the backseat, trying to keep at least a few inches between her body and big bear-guy's rolls of fat. Middle Eastern man was riding shotgun, and the third mysterious man drove.

It felt like they'd been riding on these crummy cobblestone streets for hours. But she was fairly sure it hadn't really been that long. Still, with each interminable second, all she could think about was Darin, locked in the trunk. Could he breathe back there? Was he bleeding? Throwing up?

With every bump, her heart broke. With every stop, she held her breath and listened for any sound.

Since they were now driving into Milan's city proper, her hopes had built that one of the hundreds of pedestrians milling about would recognize her distress and come to the rescue. She didn't want to think about the remoteness of such a possibility. But every street-corner cop they passed was like a symbol giving her false hope.

That hope dwindled more and more with every mile.

She closed her eyes and imagined talking to Darin in the trunk. *You are the one who needs to stay alive now. Promise me.*

A lone tear tried to escape from the corner of her eye. But Rylie never cried. Not even as a little girl. No amount of physical pain had ever been enough to bring her to tears. She had never once in her life cried over a man, either. Emotional crying seemed silly and useless. She hadn't even cried at her own father's funeral.

Sniffing back the single tear, she bit down on the inside of her cheek and thought again about the man in the trunk. *I'll find a way for us to get free if you stay alive, Darin. Trust me and hang in there. I know that as long as we're together we'll be able to master these idiots in one way or the other.*

Together.

How could she be so sure they would be able to work

together? It wasn't logical. But she was as sure of that as she was about the afternoon's sun setting in the west.

Rylie had discovered herself desperately in love for the first time in her life. Unfortunately, that life had been passing before her eyes for the last couple of hours—the way they said it did when you were about to die. Being on the edge of death had made the truth of her feelings become clear and sharp.

It didn't matter how long she and Darin had known each other. It didn't matter that they came from different parts of the world, or had vastly different backgrounds.

She loved Darin Kadir. Would always love him. Right to the last breath she ever took.

Exhaling on the prayer that she and Darin would have many more breaths to come, Rylie opened her eyes. Their car had stopped in the middle of a traffic jam. She glanced out the glass beside her and saw a man in the next car studying her. He wasn't anyone she had ever seen before, though the man seemed to recognize her.

Rylie widened her eyes and mouthed the word *help!* But what else could she do to make him understand? She let her eyes plead with him for comprehension. Then she inched her hands up to the glass to show him the ties.

Middle Eastern man in the front seat must've noticed something amiss because he spoke to bear-guy right then in a voice that sounded like a growl. The large man suddenly wrapped a beefy arm around her head and pulled her away from the window, muttering something under his breath.

With her head locked between his biceps and dense chest, she couldn't breathe and struggled for freedom. But nothing she did made a bit of difference against the wall of tubby flesh holding her tight. As she was about to pass out, the car rolled forward and bear-guy released her.

Sucking in air, she leaned back and sneaked a peek out the window. Both the man and his car were gone. Had she only dreamed them? Maybe she'd been wishing for help badly enough that any curious stranger was starting to look like a rescuer.

Their car made two more quick turns and within moments pulled into an alley behind an old four-story apartment house. Car doors opened and fresh air streamed in. Bear-guy jerked her out of the backseat and hustled her into the building.

What about Darin? She dug in her heels, trying to hang back and see if he came out of the trunk alive. But bear-guy dragged her behind him up the stairs. When she slipped once on the rough concrete steps, he just lifted her over one shoulder and thumped up the four flights with no trouble.

Next thing she knew, she was unceremoniously thrown into a tall, dark wardrobe. The door slammed shut behind her, locking the light out and her in.

Fruitlessly, she banged a fist against the wood, crying dry, silent tears for the man she loved.

Darin. Oh, Darin. Please be alive!

Darin came out of the car's trunk dizzy from the carbon monoxide and blinded by the bright sunlight. His knees buckled when he tried to stand, but one of the kidnappers wrapped a firm hand around his arm and held him upright.

Gulping in fresh air, Darin fought to clear both his lungs and his eyes. His first thought was of Rylie, and as he came to his senses, he scanned the area looking for her.

"Inside, dog. Our employer wishes to speak to you."

He tried to jerk his arm free, but received a hand across the face for his trouble. Still, he was able to scan the area around him and check out the parked car. It was empty now.

Darin experienced perhaps the worst moment of terror in his entire life. Had they killed Rylie in Bellinzona and left her body behind?

His shoulders slumped at the thought. If Rylie was gone, there would be no reason left for him to live. Let the Taj Zabbar torture him. But if he died, he would be taking a few more Taj Zabbar pigs along with him.

The henchman who'd yet to speak dragged Darin into an old building. Judging from the size of the buildings around him, the city had to be Milan. There weren't any other cities as large in all of northern Italy, and Darin knew he hadn't been driven around in that airless trunk for more than a couple of hours. In fact, another half an hour locked inside there and he might not have emerged alive at all.

"Up the stairs, Kadir." The man dressed in robes, who seemed to be in charge, held a gun to his side.

These were not regular Taj Zabbar warriors. They did not wear the Taj Zabbar colors. He and Rylie had been assaulted by a specially trained set of agents. True, they spoke in a Taj Zabbar dialect, but it was one he did not recognize.

By the fourth flight of stairs, Darin was practically crawling. Every square inch of his body hurt, but he lacked the will to care.

Rylie. They had never gotten the chance to talk. He'd never told her how much his time with her had meant. How changed he felt by knowing her. If she were really dead and a way could be found to take revenge against her killers, Darin would stay alive long enough to take it.

Did he have any hope of that? He thought of his brothers. He thought of Tarik, the undercover expert, and suddenly he could actually feel his brother's presence nearby.

He had hope.

At the top of the stairs, Darin was shoved through the door to an apartment larger than he would have thought possible from the outside. He landed on his knees on a dusty flower-patterned carpet.

The shoes of a large man appeared by his side. When he glanced up, he was looking at the visage of one of the Taj Zabbar's most important elders. Darin wasn't sure of the man's name, but he recognized him from pictures. Besides, there could be no mistaking his position from the clothes he wore. The expensive suit. The purple-checked head scarf. Even the tie imprinted with the Taj Zabbar snake and staff said this man was a leader.

"Put him in a chair," the elder ordered. "Tie him and then fetch water. We want him able to communicate, don't we?"

When his orders had been carried out, the elder stood towering over him with his hands on his hips. "You are in the presence of Sheik Newaf Bin Hamad Taj Zabbar, elder of clan Zabbar and wizeer to thousands. And you are known as Darin Kadir, eldest son of the chicken thief called Khalid Ben Shareef Kadir. No need for further introductions between us. I have come to know you well over the last few days, Kadir."

"What have you done with Rylie Hunt?"

Hamad Taj Zabbar put his hand to his chin in thought. "I can see that you are concerned. The woman is safe— temporarily. But I wish to have a calm discussion with you before the two of you are reunited. Agree?"

Rylie was still alive. Relief poured out of his pores like sweat.

Darin raised his chin and nodded sharply.

"Fine. Then the first question concerns the Hunt woman. Why did she come to Geneva? Are you and she in a...relationship...as they say in America?"

Darin wasn't sure of the right answer. Yes, of course they were in a relationship, and chances were good that the Taj Zabbar intelligence already knew it. But then why the question?

"Yes, we are in a relationship," he told Hamad, the elder. "Why have you been trying to kidnap her?"

Lights twinkled in the elder's eyes for an instant. Then he waggled a finger at Darin.

"*My* questions, Kadir. Not yours."

Hamad looked away a moment and brushed at an imaginary piece of lint on his sleeve. "You are apparently a master at covert relationships. There was not a breath of scandal about the two of you before Geneva. I am impressed."

So. The Taj Zabbar had been keeping tabs on the Kadirs. Or at least on him. Interesting.

Darin shrugged and kept his mouth shut.

"Now for the most important question. Where did you hide the Taj Zabbar property you stole?"

Darin shrugged again and fought a grin.

"No answer?" Hamad turned and gestured to one of his men. "Well then, let's see if we can make a trade. Your people take great pride in being traders, do they not?"

The elder's henchman disappeared through a door into another room. Darin heard a slight commotion coming from that direction and then a soft feminine cry.

Rylie!

He twisted in his chair, struggling against his bonds. "Don't touch her, you pig!"

The corners of Hamad's lips came up in an evil approximation of a wry smile. But the elder said nothing more until his man dragged Rylie, kicking and screaming, into the room.

"Quiet down, Miss Hunt. Your companion would like to see you."

"Darin!" Rylie's struggles turned frantic but the silent henchman held her arms and kept her steady at about ten feet away. "You're alive. Are you hurt?"

Blood had crusted over the wound on her neck and a rust-colored stain had dried on the shirt over her rib cage. It was all Darin could do not to cry out for vengeance.

Instead, he tempered his voice and spoke quietly, gently. "Shush, my darling. Say nothing. Remember your promise and trust me."

Rylie bit her lip and her eyes clouded over.

"How touchingly romantic."

At the sound of Hamad's voice, Darin turned his head to find the elder had produced an ancient Taj Zabbar dagger with a panther carved into the hilt. Its silver tip gleamed in the sunlight streaming through the glass panels of a floor-to-ceiling door out to a tiny balcony.

Hamad waved the sharp blade closer to Rylie, while her narrowed eyes were shooting daggers of hatred right back at him. "Have no fear, Miss Hunt. It is not necessary for you to learn the true significance of the Taj Zabbar Panther of Death. Our business is with the Kadir dog."

"Don't touch her," Darin growled.

No matter what it took, Darin vowed to kill this elder for causing Rylie pain. His brain churned with ideas for escape.

The elder touched the point of his blade to Rylie's cheek. "Pretty skin. It would be a shame to mar such perfection."

"I thought we were going to trade," Darin said, hoping to bring the elder's attention back to him.

"Oh, but we are trading. I am offering to keep Miss Hunt's skin in one piece in trade for the return of my own property. More than fair, don't you think?"

"Don't give him anything, Darin." Rylie was whispering, but her meaning was loud and clear. "He's going to kill us both anyway."

Darin couldn't look at her. He needed to stay strong— for her sake.

"Not if he wants his property back intact." Darin stared into Hamad's rage-filled eyes. "Okay, here's the deal I'm willing to make. I will go alone to pick up your papers. After I have them in hand, you will let Miss Hunt go in a public place of my choosing. When I see that she is safe, I will return them to you."

"Darin, no! He'll kill you."

Hamad ignored Rylie's outburst. Darin knew the elder

was no fool. He must understand that Darin was offering to sacrifice himself to save her.

"Almost a deal, Kadir. With a few minor adjustments in my favor."

The elder Hamad glanced over his shoulder to the bank of computers set up in the next room, then returned his attention to Darin. "One of my men will accompany you. You did not think I should be stupid enough to set you free to roam around Italy and contact police?

"My man will carry a phone with a camera built inside. He will take a photo of one of the pages you recover and send it to me. When I am satisfied that it is indeed my property, you may accompany him back here for the trade."

"Darin, no."

Darin shook his head at Rylie but never took his eyes off Hamad. "Not quite." Darin knew Hamad's offer had only been a first round and the man was waiting for a new bid. "Your man can come with me. But I will carry the phone. I will send a photo *and* directions for where we shall make the exchange once you send a return photo showing that Rylie is still safe and in one piece."

"I assume my property is in Milan and in a public place, yes?"

"Yes. It's still on the train like I told your idiot employees. A member of the Kadir clan does not lie."

Hamad's eyes filled with rage for a second, but he let it pass. "Very well. We will do it your way. But do not try to swindle me, dog. At the first sign of anything wrong, your lady here will begin losing body parts. A little skin. An ear. Then perhaps a finger or a few toes."

Hamad glared, clearly hoping to force Darin into a mistake. But Darin never flinched.

"If you so much as cause her one more moment's pain," Darin began with calm promise ringing in his words, "I shall never rest until you are a dead man. Nothing will stop me from hunting you down. You will pay here, or I promise I will make you pay throughout all eternity. I swear it by my ancestors."

Leaving Rylie behind with that bastard was the hardest thing Darin had ever done. Swallowing back his fear for her, he listened intently while Hamad's men spoke to each other in their odd dialect and prepared themselves for this mission to recover their boss's property. As difficult as it was to translate their speech, Darin hoped he'd learned enough to be prepared.

All three men who had assaulted them in Bellinzona pushed a still-tied Darin down the stairs out in front until they reached the alley. He understood that one of the men would accompany him as promised. But he also knew the other two would be tailing them, ready to attack if anything went awry.

"Are we taking the car? Shall I do the driving?" Darin wanted to push these men as far as possible, hoping for any mistake on their part.

The same man who'd seemed to be the leader of this trio in Bellinzona took a knife from his robes and slashed the ties binding Darin's hands. "You will remember that both your whore's life and her beauty are on the line as we travel through the city, Kadir."

He thrust the camera phone at Darin. "We will be taking a taxi to the train station and you shall not make one sound of protest on the trip. Do not hope to use that phone for any reason other than your bargain with our master."

Darin nodded, but said nothing. He could feel watchful eyes following his every move from the shadows in the alley. But instead of fear, he felt comforted. He was as sure of Tarik's presence nearby as he was of his growing hatred for Hamad.

Two of the Taj Zabbar men stayed behind as Darin had known they would. Their leader walked Darin to the corner and hailed a taxicab. Darin felt sure the other two men would be jumping into the parked car to follow them as soon as the taxi was out of sight.

The main street was oddly deserted at dusk. Seemingly out of nowhere, a lone taxi pulled up to the curb and Darin was unceremoniously shoved into the backseat.

As the taxi took off again, Darin straightened out and raised his head. He was surprised to see a man sitting in the front passenger seat. The man's body was turned around to face the backseat and he was holding a powerful gun in his hand. Even more surprisingly, the barrel of that weapon was pointed not at Darin but at the Taj Zabbar henchman.

That's when Darin spotted a very familiar profile sitting in the driver's seat. "Tarik. I knew you weren't too far away."

The Taj Zabbar assassin jerked and reached into his robes. But the deadly click of a safety being released in the front seat had him raising his empty hands in the air instead.

"Don't kill him," Darin warned the other two men. "I believe there's a GPS-type chip embedded under his skin that not only tells the Taj Zabbar of his location but also whether he remains alive or not."

The man in the front seat nodded and released his finger from the trigger. But he kept his weapon trained at the Taj Zabbar gunman's head.

"Good intelligence work, brother," Tarik told him. "But I guess that means your intentions are to try saving Miss Hunt. Otherwise, it wouldn't matter at all if we killed these assassins quickly and then blew away their Taj Zabbar leader with a few well-placed bombs. Dying in an explosion would bring justice for Uncle Sunnar, after all."

"As soon as Rylie is safe, you can do anything you want with these assassins. But Hamad Taj Zabbar is mine."

Tarik said nothing to that but kept his eyes on the road ahead.

"How'd you locate us?"

"The Taj Zabbar use ordinary cell-phone technology." Tarik shook his head at the thought. "Not the brightest move for people who are supposedly familiar with technology."

Tarik shrugged and went on. "We intercepted their calls with little trouble. Then when we had their location pinned down within a mile or two, I sent out as many men as I could find to scour the area. One of them spotted Miss Hunt riding in the backseat of their car and we followed it to their new headquarters. I have to hand it to her, she is both brave and smart."

"Drive to the train station as fast as you can," Darin quickly interjected. "I need to recover those Taj Zabbar papers and get back here in a hurry to save her."

Tarik turned the taxi down a side street, pulled to

the curb and let it idle. "Not necessary. I've already recovered the Taj Zabbar's papers. Good work on hiding them, by the way."

"How did you find them behind the padded wallpaper in our sleeping car?" Darin was astounded. "I'm absolutely positive they couldn't be spotted. I even used toothpaste to glue the quilting back down good and tight so no one would notice it had been disturbed. Not even the Taj Zabbar's best men would ever have found them there."

"Like I said," Tarik said with a chuckle, "good work. But remember it was me who taught you that trick. Those papers are on their way to headquarters right now. We'll have them decoded within days. You're a hero."

"What?" Darin felt a thrust of real panic for the first time since he'd known Tarik had come to their rescue. "Those papers aren't in Milan? How fast can you get them back here?"

"They've been in the air for a good hour. So at least that long. Maybe an hour more for the return trip. Why?"

"You may have just sealed Rylie's fate. Without those papers, she's as good as dead."

Chapter 13

"Are you comfortable?" Hamad stood beside Rylie, close enough that she could smell his spicy aftershave.

The stink made her gag. He'd had her shoved into a back bedroom and tied to a chair the same way he'd done to Darin.

"Oh, fine and dandy, thanks." Her neck wound was beginning to itch. The ties binding her hands behind her back were too flippin' tight. She was hot and hungry and nearly hysterical with worry over Darin. But she would never give this bastard the satisfaction of saying so.

"You think I am asking only to be mean? You think I am evil?" A look of concern crossed his face. "Not true, Miss Hunt. I have a proposition to make, and I believe you must be clearheaded to consider what I say."

"What kind of a proposition?"

Hamad pulled another chair close and sat down

beside her. "You are a smart woman, which is easy to see. And may I say, very beautiful, too. You could do many things in your lifetime. Profitable things."

Rylie glared at him, wondering what came next.

"It would be a shame to see your life cut short and all that potential destroyed."

"I couldn't agree more."

Hamad's leer widened. A little drool began dripping from the corner of one lip. "See there? Smart. Not like your friend the Kadir dog. He and his kind are not smart. And they shall perish for their stupidity."

It was all she could do not to spit in his face. But she didn't figure making the man mad would get her anywhere. Hamad seemed ready to propose some kind of deal. Perhaps another bid for freedom for her and Darin? Whatever it was, it could mean a chance to get out of here.

That's all Rylie wanted. A chance to free herself and save Darin. So she kept her mouth shut and listened.

"We both know that your friend will not live to see another sunrise."

"But you made him a deal," she blurted. "Why should I believe anything you have to say if you're just going to lie?"

Hamad gave her another leer along with a low chuckle. "The deal I made with him was for your life—not his. But I never had any intention of harming you." He reached over and tenderly drew his finger down her cheek.

Disgusted, she jerked her head away from his hand.

"Well, yes, perhaps you are right," he said with a

shake of his head. "It is never wise to play with your work."

"What's your proposition?" Rylie's stomach churned as the bile rose in her throat.

"I have business partners and wealthy clients, men of both integrity and power, who are in the market for a wife. Your beauty and brains would fit their requirements quite nicely."

"You want to sell me?" This bastard's gall was beyond belief. "Are you nuts? Why would I ever agree to become someone's sex slave?"

Hamad tsked at her. "Do not be so hasty. No one said anything about slavery. Let me give you a few names and you'll see what I mean by powerful."

He ticked off a half a dozen names. She recognized some as leaders of third-world countries, others as major international industrialists.

Rylie could barely sit still. She fidgeted in her seat, tugged on her ties and pursed her lips. "All right. Go on."

"I propose we hold a marriage auction. Bids to start at...say...twenty million U.S. dollars. Proceeds from the auction will be split between us."

The man wanted to auction her off to the highest bidder? He was insane. But she still needed to humor him. She had to get free, and this might provide her best chance.

"What good would that much money do for me if I ended up a slave anyway?" She could barely speak in a civil voice.

"Stop talking about slavery. Leave it to me to choose the bidders wisely. None of my clients would harm you. In fact, we would make them sign a marital contract in advance. A contract giving you both considerable freedom and a generous portion of their estate."

Estates? Now Rylie was beginning to get the picture.

"So," she began as her mind put two and two together. "If something were to happen to my new husband. Say for instance, if he died suddenly after the marriage…"

"Then you would be a very wealthy and powerful woman."

"And terribly grateful to you for putting me in that position?"

"Of course."

One of Hamad's men stuck his head in the room then and spoke in that dialect Darin had said was the Taj Zabbar language.

Hamad spit out what seemed like a curse, and then turned back to her. "You must pardon me for a few minutes, Miss Hunt. It appears that excuse for a man you find so attractive is trying a double cross. His taxi has stopped on a side street. I would guess that he is trying to bribe my employee. However, the dog will be sorely surprised on that account."

"You don't think your employee can be bribed?"

Hamad actually grinned. "Someday I will explain the special training my employees receive. They are known as assassins and fanatics, and they would rather cut off their appendages than go against their master. Each of them has already lost a toe or a finger to prove their loyalty. So, no, Miss Hunt. I am sure that my employee will not be bribed by a Kadir."

"They cut off their own fingers and toes?" Ewww. Rylie was horrified at the notion.

"I can be a most appreciative master for such loyalty."

He withdrew his knife, stepped behind her and cut the ties binding her hands. "See how kind I can be? I want you to think about our partnership without discomfort."

Hamad started to leave, but turned back at the door. "Please take this time to consider my offer. I have ordered a pleasant supper if you would be generous enough to join me. The food should arrive in about an hour—after your friend has retrieved my property and met his end. We shall talk further about our partnership then."

With those horrid words, Hamad left the room and shut the door behind him. Rylie rubbed at her arms to force the circulation back into limbs that had fallen asleep.

In a few seconds, she tried standing and shook out the kinks in her legs. The next thing she did was run to the window to look for a way out. The glass doors of the window ran from the floor almost to the ceiling and she could fling them wide-open for air. But that would be as far as she could go. The window was four flights straight up. Below was a narrow residential side street with cars parallel-parked down one side. Clearly there wouldn't be any escaping that way.

Turning a full three-sixty, she studied every inch of the room where she was being held a prisoner. One window. One door. One bed. Two chairs, a lighted wall sconce and a table. Nothing to help her escape, or that could be used to attack her jailer.

She felt useless. Tied without ropes. Nothing to use as a weapon.

With at least three large Taj Zabbar men, she was outnumbered and overpowered physically. Her brains

were all she had left with which to defend herself.
And right this minute she couldn't think of anything
that might help. Darin was the one and only thought
occupying her mind. She might get out of here in one
piece by using her wits, but what about him? Damn it.
They were a team now. He couldn't die. How could she
let that happen?

Standing at the open window, she kicked furiously
and hit nothing but air. Sighing, she looked out over
the Milan rooflines, just beginning to disappear in the
dusk settling over the labyrinth of city buildings. From
here she caught a glimpse of the Castello Sforzesco.
A place she knew as a historic castle, located on a
marvelous piazza that made for good photographs. Rylie
remembered it from having been in Milan once before
with her parents—years ago as a teenage tourist.

The fleeting thought of her parents brought a familiar
ache. Her father would've known how to get out of a
mess like this. But Rylie was stumped. Aware that for
the first time in her life she was in a situation that she
couldn't control, Rylie sank down on the bed.

She thought of Darin. The first man she had ever
truly loved with her whole heart. The only man other
than her father that she could envision as a partner. But
in Darin's case, it was as a partner for life.

Rylie yearned for him. The two of them had never
gotten their chance to talk. Or to just be together. And
now she had no way of helping him, either. He was out
there somewhere, fighting to save her life. And here she
was, a useless puppet with no way out. She had always
been a fighter, and the frustration of being boxed in
weighed heavily on her chest.

Staring bleakly out at the first of the evening stars,

she had to swipe at her cheeks as tears began to roll. Useless. Out of control. Boxed in.

She thought of her mother. Of the others back at home who still needed her help when she couldn't even help herself. More tears threatened. Defeat settled in around her shoulders like a shawl.

Finally she threw herself across the bed and sobbed. A fountain of liquid pain erupted from somewhere deep inside. Her tears appeared at first because of the frustrating situation. But they quickly turned into a waterfall of the unshed grief that she had refused to express for the last six months.

Oh, Daddy, I miss you. I'm so sorry to let you down but I can't do this one alone. For the first time ever, I admit I need help and now no one is there to come save me.

Below the window, standing in the growing shadows, Darin and his brother looked up at the light as Rylie's image had moved in and then back out of view.

"Miss Hunt doesn't look much like a prisoner to me." Tarik spoke in soft voice.

"She is." Darin could feel Rylie's frustration and desperation in the same way as he had felt Tarik's presence earlier.

Speaking quietly to his brother over his shoulder, he said, "Are you sure that assassin is still alive and on his way to the train station?" Darin was smart enough to match Tarik's low whispers.

"Positive. As we tied him and put him in the taxi's trunk, he attempted suicide, but we were too quick for him. We also took care of his pals, the ones in the car following the taxi."

"We have to get Rylie out of there soon." Darin's anxiety was growing as the minutes ticked by. "Before Hamad realizes I don't have access to his papers."

Tarik turned to face him. "I've had a thought about that, bro. There might be another trick that'll give us the few extra minutes we need to form a rescue plan."

It was all Darin could do to drag his gaze away from the fourth-story window where he knew Rylie was being held. "What is it? We don't have a lot of time for preparations. That taxi will be pulling in to the train station at any moment."

"No need for long, drawn-out preparations." Tarik was studying his face in the low light coming from a nearby second-story window. "We only need your ability to carry out a covert story line. How are you at lying?"

A flash of his earlier smart-assed reply to Hamad about Kadirs not lying ran through Darin's mind. But the thought was quickly replaced by a picture of Rylie's face in the throes of passion. What if he could never see that spectacular look of pleasure ever again? Hell, he couldn't lose her now. That she'd landed in this mess in the first place was all his fault.

"I can lie when necessary," he said slowly.

"Uh-huh."

"Tell me what you want me to do, Tarik. I'll do anything."

Tarik sighed. "You really love her, don't you? I've never seen you respond to a woman this way before."

"Tell me."

Tarik was carrying a high-tech toy in a pocket and it buzzed twice, then stopped. "That's the signal. The taxi has arrived at the station. You have to do this now. Put in a call to Hamad like you promised. But tell him the train is surrounded by cops and you can't reach the sleeping car. Tell him he has to give you more time. Another hour so that you can find a way past the police."

It might work and was worth a try.

Darin took a deep breath and pulled Hamad's cell phone from his pocket. "He doesn't have a way of locating me from this phone, does he?"

Tarik chuckled. "Naw. I pulled the GPS chip, put it in a throwaway cell and put it in the taxi. These Taj dudes are seriously screwy. It's like they have one foot in the twenty-first century and one foot in the Middle Ages. Make the call."

Darin punched the single phone button like Hamad had shown him. When the bastard answered, Darin gave him the lie and even managed to bluff a line about why there wasn't any background noise in the train station.

After he hung up, Darin didn't feel as elated over making Hamad believe the story as he'd thought he should. He hadn't been able to talk to Rylie, and they still needed a plan to free her. He wasn't going to feel anything good until she was back by his side.

"Nice work, brother."

The new voice had Darin whirling around. "Shakir! How did you sneak up on me? What are you doing here?"

"I move quietly." Shakir's understatement almost made Darin grin. "And you don't think I would let my two brothers have all the fun, do you?"

"I'm not sure *fun* would be the word for attacking a Taj Zabbar stronghold."

Shakir patted him on the shoulder. "Now, now. Thus far, I've been enjoying myself immensely. I took down the three outside Taj Zabbar guards a few moments ago. Well, with help from one of Tarik's men. And I found that action to be bloody brilliant."

Shakir rubbed his hands together. "So, what's the plan for reaching the fourth floor?"

Tarik had been speaking softly into a hidden mouthpiece, but at his brother's question, he turned back. "Our intel shows there's possibly three more guards inside the apartment, along with Hamad and the girl. We don't have a plan yet."

"And you're sure we can't just blow up the whole freakin' building?" Shakir looked gleeful at the idea.

Darin rolled his eyes and ignored the comment. "We have to go with what we know. We know Rylie is in that back bedroom. A few moments ago, she was alone. I can reach her room from the roof. While I'm doing that…"

"Hold it." Tarik held up his palms. "What exactly do you mean by 'reach her room from the roof'?"

Both of his brothers were staring at him as if he'd suddenly sprouted angel wings.

"It's not that big a distance from the roof to the top of her open window. Maybe one of Tarik's men can lower me down with some kind of makeshift rope."

"You're crazy, Darin." Tarik was shaking his head.

"Lovesick is more like it." Shakir's head was rolling side to side, as well.

"Nonsense," Darin insisted. "This can work. You two attack through the front door and make a big commotion. Use flash bangs or something. Everyone's attention will be drawn your way while I climb down and protect Rylie until the attack is over and the Taj Zabbar are finished."

"I thought you wanted to be the one to kill Hamad Taj Zabbar?" Tarik was looking at him thoughtfully.

"Rylie's safety is more important."

Tarik looked to Shakir. The two of them shrugged and then released their breaths as one.

"Okay, Darin, we'll go with your plan. But one of my men will cover you from the roof across the street. In case."

Darin started to argue with Tarik that it wasn't necessary, but the determined looks on his brothers' faces made him shut his mouth. He knew to quit while he was ahead.

What he didn't know was how Rylie was holding up. Fighting terror-filled images and dreadful thoughts of what Hamad was doing to her, Darin prepared himself to be her savior. But what kind of shape would she be in when he came to her rescue?

Rylie forced down another bite of filet mignon, but her stomach was churning with acid already. Light-headed and suddenly too warm, she twisted around to check that the bedroom window was still open. It was, but not a breath of air stirred in the room.

"The food is good, yes?" Hamad sat across the table from her and had been silently concentrating on his meal for the last ten minutes. "I must apologize again for the unforeseen problems keeping us from discussing our plans over this excellent meal. Though I completely understand. Certainly you would not feel free to contemplate a future while your *friend* is still breathing.

"But do not overly concern yourself," he added

flippantly. "That little detail should be rectified shortly."

Hamad took another sip of his burgundy wine and stared at her over the two-person table he'd had erected in the bedroom, allowing them to eat in private. "I'm sure it will be only a matter of an hour, more or less. Perhaps the announcement of his end shall arrive while we're having brandy. And then we can be free to discuss our partnership."

Rylie shifted the steak knife into her right hand and pretended to use it to cut her meat like the Europeans. As far as weapons went, the little knife wasn't much. Certainly no match for Hamad's antique dagger or his bodyguards' guns. She would have to get too close to an opponent for it to do any good.

Still, she didn't feel nearly as helpless with a knife in her hand as she had without one. The mere sight of it had been one of the reasons she had agreed to sit down at this table with a person who seemed mad.

Relieved to find out Darin was still alive, she would have agreed to almost anything when Hamad suggested they should eat the meal he'd had prepared while they waited to hear something more from the train station. Since then, her mind had raced with escape plans as she listened to Hamad sounding more and more deranged.

He talked to her as if they were having a business meeting. As if the two of them were on the same side. And as if Darin's life was only a stubborn detail to be negotiated between them.

Hmm. Was that a possibility?

"Sheik Hamad, may I ask a question?"

He waved a good-natured hand in her direction. "Of course."

"You said before that people who were loyal to you could expect your appreciation. Would that be true of me, as well?"

Nodding, he stuffed his mouth with creamy pasta.

"What if I agreed to every one of your ideas, and in addition signed a contract letting you manage all my money from now on? Would you consider me a loyal partner then?"

He dropped his fork and grinned, ignoring the ring of Alfredo-style sauce around his mouth. "You would make me ecstatically happy, my dear. And could expect me to be most appreciative."

She steeled herself for his reaction to her next statement. "I will do all that as fast as it can be arranged. Tonight if possible. But in return, I would need your promise that Darin Kadir will be kept alive."

Hamad pushed back from the table and stood. "Whore! You try to trick me?"

Rylie also stood. But she rose on shaky legs and backed up a few steps.

"It's n-not a trick," she stuttered. "Only a business deal."

"The Kadir clan must all die. *All.* Darin Kadir cannot be an exception. It is preordained." Hamad took his dagger from an inside pocket and shook it menacingly as he came in her direction. "No more talking. I will ask for your decision once again after the Kadir dog is dead. By then we'll see what you have to say."

Hanging on to her steak knife like a lifeline, Rylie expected to feel the blade of Hamad's dagger at any moment. But if the cut came, she swore to do her own damage in return.

All of a sudden Hamad's eyes grew wide as he stared

over her shoulder toward the window at her back. She hesitated to turn around for fear he would stab her from behind.

"Stop. Or I will cut her." Hamad raised his dagger over his head.

A big arm came around her waist then and dragged her sideways into a solid, masculine chest. Without looking, Rylie immediately knew it was Darin. Her heart started up again. It hadn't really been beating since she'd last seen him. Now she could breathe. He was alive.

Darin pulled her backward until they hit a solid wall. "Stay away from the window," he whispered in her ear.

Something whizzed through the window next to her. A bullet? But it missed the agitated Hamad, who was stepping from side to side.

At that very moment, a huge commotion began in the next room. Explosions rang out. Men shouted. The door opened and one of Hamad's men ran into the room brandishing a firearm and shouting curses in his own language. Then the assassin fired a wild shot and screamed like a banshee.

Darin stepped in front of her and used his body as a shield. But she didn't want his protection. She wanted to work with him to take out Hamad and get free. They were a team.

Smoke filled the room, and Rylie lost track of things in the confusion. She slid out from behind Darin and came face-to-face with Hamad's bodyguard.

His huge knife gleamed at her through the haze. Darin yelled something Rylie couldn't understand. She wanted to turn and ask him for a better weapon than her silly steak knife, but she was afraid to lose sight of their attacker.

The assassin kept coming—closer and closer to both her and Darin. By now all she could see through the smoky haze was their attacker's yellowed teeth. It was surreal.

And Rylie knew that meant they didn't have much time left.

Chapter 14

The smoke from his brothers' flash bangs grew thicker. Darin could see that Tarik's sniper wouldn't be able to get off another clear shot while smoke poured from the window. Good thing, because Rylie had disappeared into obscurity somewhere near that same window. He should've known Rylie wouldn't cower behind him in a fight.

But how was he supposed to protect her when she wouldn't stand still? He suddenly caught sight of her through the haze. And his heart stopped. On hold—along with his breathing. She had a small knife in her hand and was waving it slowly in front of her as though the puny blade would be a major deterrent to any attacker.

"Rylie, duck and cover." He tried to get her attention, but she seemed frozen in the midst of chaos.

She wasn't too far away from him. But smoke blew

between them again and she disappeared. He took a couple of steps forward, hoping that she would still be in the same spot.

Darin pulled his weapon but was terrified to use it for fear of hitting Rylie—or maybe of hitting one of his brothers. Where were his brothers? Perhaps they had run into more trouble than they'd expected in the front room.

The smoke began lifting. But it still flowed out the window, obscuring the sniper's clear shot from across the street.

"No!" That was Hamad's voice, suddenly ringing out loud and clear. "Not her. Do not harm that one."

Darin finally saw Rylie, turning to the sound of shouting. With his heart bursting in his chest, Darin turned his head, too, and saw Hamad standing on the opposite side of a dinner table with his back to the door. The Taj elder must've closed and locked the door between the bedroom and the front room to let the smoke clear. But Darin knew that wouldn't slow his Kadir brothers down for long.

He swung back to find Rylie. She stood not far away with her back to him. She was facing one of Hamad's assassins. The man appeared to be stalking her with dagger in hand.

"Rylie!"

Hamad started screaming orders once again. "That one! Kill the man. Kill the Kadir dog!"

Things seemed to happen in slow motion from then on. Both the assassin and Rylie lifted their heads to look for Darin. Meanwhile, Darin took a step or two closer to them.

The assassin reared his arm back and let his dagger

fly. Rylie screamed, dropped her knife and threw herself at Darin—stepping right into the flight path of the dagger.

Darin could visualize what was going to happen before the dagger ever hit her in the back. But he was helpless to do anything. Time stopped. It was like the worst horror show he had ever seen, and he knew it would haunt his nightmares forever.

Rylie's eyes opened wide as the knife buried itself deep in her flesh. She took another step forward and hesitated. A look of confusion crossed her face. Darin caught her up with his one free arm.

"No. You idiot! Kill the Kadir!" Hamad was still shouting but he didn't move from his spot of safety across the room.

Darin turned, pointed and fired his gun, hitting Hamad right in the forehead. The look of shock on the Taj Zabbar elder's face was priceless. He opened his mouth automatically but then puffed out his lips and looked like a fish out of water, gulping for air. The very next instant, Hamad dropped to the floor like a heap of trash.

Still holding on to Rylie, Darin turned his gun and pointed it at the assassin. The startled man stared at his boss on the floor for a split second. Then the assassin pulled a stiletto from his own shoe. With his pulse beating wildly, Darin once again prepared to fire.

But the assassin was quicker. Without a second's hesitation, he used the knife to slit his own throat. A horrific sight. Blood spouted like a fountain from the man's neck, and it was over before Darin could pull the trigger.

"Is it finished? Are we safe?" Rylie managed to

speak in a weak voice. But when Darin nodded, her legs collapsed from under her.

"I knew we made a good team." Rylie's eyes closed as she grew limp against him. Letting loose of his weapon, he pulled her into his arms and together they sank to the carpet.

"Hang on, Rylie. Just hang on." Trembling, Darin rocked her in his arms.

Hold on, my love. She couldn't die now. It would kill him to know another woman he loved had died because of him. If she died, he died.

Tarik and Shakir broke through the door.

"Hey, bro, no fair. You managed all this without us. Where's the fun in that?"

"You're sure she's going to live?" Darin had asked that same question of various doctors at least a thousand times over the last three days.

"Miss Hunt was extremely lucky." Rylie's newest specialist spoke in one of those serious doctor's voices everyone always hated.

But as the specialist turned to her in the bed, he offered up a bit of genuine cheer. "The knife blade missed most of your vital organs but just nicked your liver. You're going to be with us for a while, but when you leave the hospital you should be able to resume your regular activities."

It was all Darin could do not to kiss the man. The warm flow of relief poured through his body all at once, forcing him to sit down. He leaned his elbows on his knees and put his head in his hands.

When the doctor said his goodbyes and left them alone, Rylie spoke. "Are you feeling okay, Darin? You don't look well. You're sure you don't have any internal injuries?"

He raised his head and looked over at her. "I'm sure. The doctors tell me I have a bruised kidney, but that I should heal with no trouble. Other than that, I guess I look worse than I feel."

"Purple and green splotches seem to suit you."

She was making jokes. He felt as though the end of the world was right around the corner and she was making jokes.

Standing, he went to her bedside and gazed down on her. "Yeah? Well, you look beautiful, too. All quiet and regal lying in that bed. Like a sleeping beauty."

She did look beautiful. Beautiful and fragile and slightly shell-shocked over what they'd been through. He hadn't seen her looking this vulnerable since the night they'd met when she'd been jet-lagged and scared.

He'd done that to her. Made her vulnerable again.

Everything that had happened to her, brushing her with death and this hospital stay was his fault. He felt helpless again.

Rylie reached out, her hand encumbered by needles and wires, and touched him. He gently took her fingers with his own. Their connection was immediate.

He experienced her warmth. Her gentleness. The spark of life that still burned strongly within her heart.

His obsession with her was as vivid as ever. He longed to hold her. To make love to her. To keep her with him always.

But every time he looked at her, he also remembered the stark terror he'd felt when she came toward him—the hilt of that huge dagger sticking out of her back. He would *never* forget it.

Darin couldn't keep doing this. He couldn't stay here and potentially be the reason for her coming to more harm. The Taj Zabbar were not finished with their war. They still intended to kill the Kadirs. And the next time, she might not…

"Have you talked to my mother? And to my friend Marie Claire? Do they know I'm all right?"

Swallowing down the hard lump in his throat, he said, "Your friend telephoned your mother last night and told her a story about you visiting a spa for a few days. We didn't want to worry your mother too much. You can call and talk to her yourself as soon as you're feeling well enough."

He tried a smile, but knew immediately that it was a dismal failure. "Marie Claire is taking time off from work to come visit with you while you're here. She says she wants to see for herself that you're really okay."

"It'll be nice to assure Marie Claire—and to be able to cheer up my mother again." A ghost of a smile lingered around Rylie's mouth.

Hell. This woman was amazing. She was thinking about everyone but herself.

All he could think about was how close she'd come to dying. Tears burned the backs of his eyes.

"What…" Rylie stopped to clear her throat. "What happened with the Milan police? All those…dead bodies."

Darin squeezed her fingers to let her know he understood what was going on inside her head. How seeing men die could affect you for the rest of your life.

"Don't worry. Tarik has friends in high places here in Milan. He's taking care of it."

Rylie tried to shift her body and grimaced with the effort.

"Want to sit up a little more? Here, let me adjust the bed." He used the remote to raise the head of the bed and then showed her how it worked.

"Thanks," she said when she was settled again. "Actually, thanks for everything. I wouldn't have made it out alive if not for you."

He shook his head. "Don't say that." *Please don't even think that. Without me, you wouldn't have been in the line of fire in the first place.*

"You're a strong, independent woman," he said instead of what he was thinking. "Nobody can get you down."

Her eyes clouded over with sadness. "Can you do me one more favor?"

He nodded and held his breath.

"Can you check on Hunt Drilling while I'm stuck in this hospital? See how the company is doing and how the victims of the explosion are faring. I should be there. I shouldn't have...I shouldn't have left them the way I did."

This one was easy. "I've already talked to my attorneys in Houston. Kadir Shipping will be paying all the bills related to that explosion at the Houston shipping facility. We're setting up a victims' fund, as well. I know it doesn't make up for the suffering." He shrugged but couldn't manage a smile. "Anything we can do."

"But the explosion wasn't the fault of Kadir Shipping."

If only that were true. "The Taj Zabbar would never

have noticed Hunt Drilling if not for Kadir Shipping. It's our fault and we will make amends."

Darin wished he could put her mind more at ease about her father's firm. "I've decided to publicly break our ties with Hunt Drilling. I want you and the company off the Taj Zabbar radar. But if you'd be willing, Kadir Shipping will become your company's silent partner. We'll funnel you anything you need to bring Hunt Drilling back to a place of prominence. Money. Expertise. Anything."

A light moved into her eyes for the first time since she'd been stabbed. "Thank you—again. Uh, so what you're saying is that you believe the Taj Zabbar will continue trying to kill your people, even though Hamad is dead?"

"He was only one man. Now he's a martyr. They have many that would gladly die like him if it meant doing harm to the Kadirs."

She tilted her head in thought the way he'd seen her do before. He tried to memorize the movement for the coming endless nights without her.

"Then you and your brothers intend to continue with your secret actions in order to stop the Taj Zabbar?" she asked at last. "You still plan on proving to the international community that they're the bad guys."

"Yes, certainly. Nothing has really changed."

"You know," she began, sounding almost coy. "Hamad gave me information regarding his operation. I could potentially be a big help in your investigations."

And there it was. Exactly what he had been dreading. Her first move to talk about their future.

He didn't know what kind of story would be the best way to go, but he wanted to let her down gently. Should he pretend he didn't care? Shrug her off and say, "It's been fun, but…"

Rylie would never buy that. She was far too smart, and he had been far too open about how much she meant to him.

No, he had no choice but to stay with who he was. Stay with the honest truth.

He steeled himself, drew in a deep breath and began, "Rylie, my life has become—complicated. Dangerous. Far too dangerous to be starting any new…uh… relationships. At every turn, I run the risk of being killed. By a sniper—a knife attack—or by an explosion."

Her face paled at the mention of explosions, but he was in too deep to stop now. "I can't afford to take on any obligations at this point. It's not…"

"But we're a team," she said softly. "I'm not an obligation. I can help. I want to help. The Taj Zabbar are truly evil and they need to be stopped."

"Not by you." The words came rushing out of his mouth too harshly, but he was becoming frustrated. Frustrated and devastated.

"Look," he began again after composing himself. "Your company needs you. Go back and take over. I'll send Tarik here to the hospital to take your statement before you leave. Tell him what you know. And let us do the rest. Stay away from the Taj Zabbar."

"Darin, please." Her voice wavered, cracking as she spoke his name.

Turning his head rather than look at her didn't help.

She insisted, "You know what I'm asking. I realize we've only known each other for a week, but what about us? I thought we had…a thing. Where do we go from here?"

"We don't go anywhere." He hung his head, still unable to look her in the eye. "At the risk of sounding clichéd, there is no *we*. You don't have any idea what you're asking. There can't be anything between us as long as the Taj Zabbar continues their war against the Kadirs."

"But…"

He couldn't take any more. Knowing he was hurting her was killing him.

"I'd better let you get some rest." He moved toward the door without turning to face her.

"You're not coming back, are you?"

He stopped, hesitated, but knew he couldn't weaken now. "You're going to be fine. Your girlfriend should arrive in a couple of hours. You two sure don't need me hanging around."

"Darin, wait…" Her words were interrupted by the saddest-sounding sob he had ever heard.

And without ever turning around, Darin did the hardest thing he had ever done in his entire life. He walked out the door.

"Damn, but it's bloody dark in this place." Shakir walked to the window and threw open the drapes. "And your apartment is utterly disgusting. Where the hell have you been, brother? We haven't even seen your shadow for weeks."

"I needed some time off." Darin slammed down his beer bottle and put his feet up on the desk. "And I don't remember asking for your opinion about my housekeeping, little brother."

Shakir walked to the sofa, brushed aside the empty liquor bottles and remnants of peanut shells, and sat down. "Bugger that. You never needed a vacation before."

Picking up a half-empty bottle, Shakir stared as liquid pooled on the carpeting. "Why the sudden need for booze? You seldom drink."

"I do now." Darin looked over at his brother and shook his head. "You and Tarik have been talking about me, haven't you?"

"We might have." Shakir put the bottle on the table and rested his elbows on his knees. He leaned forward, ready to have his say while looking sincere.

Oh, no. Here came the "get your act together" speech. Darin turned his back and stared out the window at the sun shining against the crystal-blue Mediterranean. How he hated that sight. The color reminded him of the sexy eyes that had been haunting his dreams. That's why he'd closed the damned drapes in the first place.

"Well, get on with it." Darin let the irritation show in his tone. "Tell me why I need to go back to work. Give me the lecture about supporting the Kadir cause."

Darin needed something, certainly. Maybe he needed his brother to kick a bit of sense into him. Darin was itching to hit something. Or pound on someone. But he was too annoyed with the world at the moment to make a move. That made him an asshole.

And his brothers were bigger asses for caring.

"No need," Shakir said. "You've got all the answers."

Darin wished he had all the answers. Or an Aladdin's lamp to give him what he wanted the most. He'd spent days drowning in his own self-pity, wishing that the Taj Zabbar would disappear off the face of the earth.

"I suppose all this—" Shakir waved a hand over the

mess in the apartment "—has something to do with Rylie Hunt. Want to talk about her?"

"Not much." He hadn't heard a word from her since the day he'd turned his back and walked out.

But what had he expected? He'd apparently done a terrific job of driving home his point. She'd be better off if she stayed thousands of miles away from him.

And yes, it hurt to think he would never see her again. So what? Love always hurt. One way or the other. But better hurt than dead.

"Tarik went to see her." Shakir sat back and Darin could feel him looking for a reaction. "Says she's real smart. She gave us several leads to follow. But we… need someone to analyze those leads."

"Was she all right?"

Shakir slowly breathed in and out until he finally said, "She was being dismissed from the hospital. Heading back to Texas as I understand."

Suddenly Darin had a terrible thought. "What if the Taj Zabbar decide to seek retribution against her for Hamad's death?" Why hadn't he been smart enough to see this possibility before?

Shakir raised his eyebrows, but spoke softly. "Something like that is always possible, but…"

"No, seriously. The Kadirs can't be in any more trouble with the Taj Zabbar than they already have been for centuries. But what about Rylie? They must know she participated in Hamad's death."

Breathing deep, Shakir'shook his head. "This is war, Darin. Covert war, but war, nevertheless. You have heard the saying, 'War is hell'? No one can be one hundred percent safe in times like these."

"But she has to be safe. She has to be."

Darin stood and began to pace. He kicked out at the newspapers and books littering his floor. *Think.*

But his thinking was hampered by the amount of alcohol in his system. He turned to his brother for help.

"Shakir, we have to protect her. She didn't ask for this. It isn't her war."

"It seems to me that our war is her war now." Shakir calmly folded his hands and followed Darin's movements with his eyes. "She stepped into it willingly. Didn't she come to Geneva looking for answers? Well, she got them."

No! Darin couldn't accept that. Wouldn't.

Feeling more useless than he ever had been in his life, Darin slumped down on a chair. "Help me. Please. Someone has to watch over her. Make sure she's not in danger."

"Someone?"

Chapter 15

Rylie threw a quick look over her shoulder and dashed for the stairs leading to her second-floor condo. *Who was that man?* There'd been a dark figure lingering at the edge of the parking lot, smoking a cigarette—and watching her.

Ohmygod.

With her heart pounding out a beat like a high-stepping marching band, she took the stairs two at a time. Grateful for having her keys already in hand, by the time Rylie hit the second-floor hallway she was already punching her house key toward the lock.

Shaking badly as she reached the door, she dropped her set of keys and had to scramble around to pick them up. Then she held her breath, unlocked the door and was inside in a blink.

Letting loose of her gym bag, she turned back,

relocked the door and set the chain. Then she leaned her head against the closed door, drew in a deep breath and listened for any out-of-place noise. Were those footsteps on the stairs? Movement just outside her door?

Rylie squeezed her eyes shut and regulated her breathing. It was okay. She was okay.

Most probably the danger had all been in her head. Still, she would be glad when tomorrow arrived and they installed the new alarm system she'd ordered.

As her heart rate slowed, she thought back to her discussion with Tarik right before she'd left the hospital. He was the one who'd put thoughts in her head of the Taj Zabbar coming after her for retribution. It had come from an offhanded comment of his. A single phrase about watching her back.

But after considering the idea for the last couple of weeks, she had to agree that it was a possibility. So possible that after getting settled back at home, she'd gone out and bought herself a new handgun. Then she'd signed up for target practice, ordered the alarm system and returned to her self-defense classes in earnest.

She sighed and figured she was being silly to worry about some strange man in the parking lot. Throwing her gym bag on the couch and heading to the kitchen, she turned on all the lights. Deciding she needed something stronger than bottled water when she opened the fridge, she dug out a diet cola. Not that she really needed to diet.

However, if she were totally being truthful, she had put on a few pounds since her return to the States. Still, no one would call her chubby. But she did figure that the carbonation in the cola would settle her still-trembling stomach and nerves.

She held the cold unopened can to her forehead and stared blankly into the fridge. Being a little frightened now and then was good for a person. Would keep her on her toes.

And working on bettering her own self-defense skills was something to do besides sitting around worrying about Darin and feeling sorry for herself. She certainly wasn't in demand at Hunt Drilling these days.

By the time she'd been released from the hospital and made it back to Midland, Darin's people had already convinced the federal investigators that the shipping-facility explosion was an act of terrorism against both Hunt Drilling and Kadir Shipping. The word had spread that Hunt's employees and executives had done nothing wrong and were victims themselves. Business was booming again from people who wanted to show their support. Not surprisingly, the loyal, longtime employees at Hunt had also stepped up in her absence, and the company had been running smoothly even before her return.

No one needed her at work anymore.

Even her mother was blooming again and didn't seem to need her much, either. True to his word, Darin's attorneys had set up a victims' assistance fund and then had called upon her mother to administer the money in the name of her deceased husband. Rachel Hunt was in her element, working long hours visiting invalids, paying off hospital bills and approving no-interest loans.

The last thing Rachel needed at this point was a mopey daughter hanging around.

Her phone jangled suddenly, causing Rylie to drop the can, just missing her toes. Squeaking, she slammed the refrigerator door and picked up the receiver while searching for calm.

"Rylie, this is Tarik Kadir. Is everything all right?"

"Tarik? Has something happened to Darin?" Her pulse stood at a standstill. Her mind blanked.

"He's fine. Maybe a little pathetic, but he's slowly coming around."

She swallowed hard, trying to keep the melancholy sound out of her voice. "What can I do for you? Why are you calling?"

"I wanted to tell you that we intercepted a Taj Zabbar directive today. They've put out a contract on your life, Rylie. They want you dead for taking part in the killing of Hamad. I've been afraid of this."

Gasping, she nearly dropped the phone. She gripped the receiver as if it were her only lifeline and listened as Tarik spoke in even tones.

"You should be okay," he added. He sounded so sure of himself that her heart rate evened out. "I've had a couple of our men watching out for you for the last week to ten days. Just in case. They tell me you're taking some smart steps toward your own safety. That's good. And, uh…"

He hesitated for only a second and then finished the thought. "Uh…I also thought you should know Darin is on his way to the States to help you with further safety precautions."

"I…see." She leaned against the counter for support instead of crumbling to her knees.

"You haven't given up on him, have you?" Tarik's voice was full of worry. "My brother, well, Darin's personality and background have given him a handicap when it comes to relationships. You should talk to him about it sometime."

She almost smiled. "You would have no way of knowing this, Tarik, but I intend to talk to him, and I don't give up easily."

"Actually, I do know about you not giving up," he admitted. "I've been checking you out. I think you might be a great addition to my investigations team. If you're interested. And if your business can stand to lose you for a while."

Chuckling at the very idea of being on a Kadir team, she asked, "Does Darin know about this?"

"Not yet. I thought I'd let you find the best way to tell him after you've thought it through and made a decision."

Rylie thanked Darin's brother for the job offer and agreed to give the idea serious consideration. It might be just the thing she'd been looking for. Especially now that she had a price on her head.

Relieved to find out that the scary guy watching her from the parking lot had been one of Tarik's men, she turned her thoughts to the other man she'd been trying to forget for weeks. *Darin* was on his way.

Wondering whether he would be coming in tonight or waiting until tomorrow morning, she decided that either way a shower was in order. She'd better wash her hair and maybe even shave her legs.

Rylie dragged her T-shirt up and over her head, leaving the sports bra for last. Moving through the condo, she grabbed her gym bag and started down the hall, turning on lights as she went.

Halfway there she thought about how heavy the gym bag had grown recently. She'd taken to carrying her twenty-pound weights in order to do some light lifting, keeping in shape at home. And it had been working.

Smiling, she wondered if Darin would appreciate how strong she'd made herself. She would have to ask him when he arrived. Of course, if she had any say in the matter, they would be doing a lot more than talking. Sex seemed to be the way they communicated the best.

The idea made her warm all over. She couldn't wait.

Ready to hit the shower, she skipped the rest of the way down the hall and pushed open her bedroom door. A Taj Zabbar assassin stood on the other side, his gigantic dagger gleaming at her in the hall's light.

Darin tried to stay under the speed limit, but the car his man had provided at the Midland airport seemed to jump right out from under him at every turn. Or maybe that was due to his lead foot and jumpy nerves making him press ever harder on the accelerator.

He couldn't tell if he was more worried about Rylie's immediate safety or about having to face her again. There might be some serious backpedaling going on the next time he saw her. He should never have left her on her own. Now he owed her a major apology.

When he'd first landed at the Midland two hours ago and cleared customs, he'd considered checking into the hotel and then going to Rylie's in the morning when they were both fresh. But something urged him to see her tonight. To finish with the apologies and start on plans for her safety.

She wasn't going to like having to hide out, moving around from one safe house to the next, maybe even changing her name. That wasn't Rylie's style. But he was here to make sure it happened. Even if she hated him for it.

Stopping for a traffic light, Darin thought about calling her. His men had reported that they'd tailed her from the gym to her apartment a little while ago. He knew she was home. But maybe she was expecting company tonight.

That errant thought did not make him very happy. He had never given a moment's consideration to the chance that she might find someone else. And he didn't like the image in his mind of her with anyone new.

But he wasn't here as her date. He was here for her safety.

He'd better call ahead. Punching in the number he had memorized but never used, Darin listened to it ring. Perhaps he would invite her out to dinner. She wouldn't feel uncomfortable about talking to him alone in a restaurant. He didn't want to push her.

Yes, the more he thought about that idea the more he liked it. They could find a nice, quiet restaurant where he would explain all the ramifications of her new status as a Taj Zabbar target for death. She couldn't become too mad in a public place, could she?

Her answering machine picked up. He left a short message and hung up. But then he suddenly knew something wasn't right. He called one of the men he had watching her place.

"Yes sir, Mr. Kadir," the guard assured him. "She went inside her condo about twenty minutes ago and she hasn't come out. Miss Hunt turned on a lot of lights and they're all still on. Maybe she's in the shower and that's why she isn't picking up her phone."

Darin swallowed back his terror long enough to tell

the man to meet him in her parking lot. Then he checked his GPS. Five more minutes to her door. He decided to make it in two.

Be safe, Rylie. I'm on the way.

When the phone rang and startled them both, Rylie flipped around and flew down the hall away from the assassin. Running in a zigzag pattern, she worked hard to avoid the repeat horror of a knife being thrust into her back. But the heavy footsteps in the carpeting right behind her said she didn't stand a chance. Her assailant apparently wasn't trying for a clear shot. This man seemed to want his assault up close and personal.

Adrenaline surged through her veins as she hit the end of the hallway and dashed around the couch in the living room, trying to put some distance between herself and the attacker. Sweating profusely, she ran faster, wanting a lead that would allow her to unlock and escape out the front door.

Too late.

On the next step, her hair was grabbed roughly from behind. The surprise move yanked her head backward and made her stop in her tracks. Ignoring the pain, she planted her feet and twisted her slick, sweaty hair free of his grasp. As she jerked and turned, she swung the gym bag as hard as she could with both hands.

Her quick move surprised the assassin, and he stumbled back a step while his dagger went sailing. She would've tried to retrieve his blade but getting out was her first impulse. The front-door locks would take too long. Heading for the utility room back door, she scrambled into the kitchen, moving her feet faster than she'd ever thought humanly possible.

But her attacker was almost as quick. She rounded the kitchen counter, heart crashing inside her chest and her goal in sight. But she wasn't watching her feet. Tripping over the cola can, she slipped on the tile. Down she went and slid headfirst into a cabinet. Pain drove through her shoulder, but she forced herself onto her knees and then blindly came to her feet.

Too late again. Her assailant had her cornered against the kitchen cabinets. The edges of his mouth came up in a terrifying grin while he withdrew a long, silken cord from his coat pocket. Pulling the cord taut between his two hands, the assassin came in her direction.

She tried to fight him off, digging her fingers at his eyes and kneeing him in the groin. But he was way too big. Overpowering.

Before she could slip away, he whipped the cord around her neck and drew it tight. Wildly thrashing about, trying to find something to use as a weapon, Rylie fought with everything she had. She used her nails against his hands, kicked backward at his knees and punched at his head. If she could plant her feet again, she might be able to leverage him over her shoulder. But her time was running out. She was already getting light-headed.

Out of nowhere the doorbell rang, once again startling the assassin as he turned his head toward the noise. Rylie used the momentary lapse to her best advantage.

She leaned closer to a drawer, ripped it open and pulled out a carving knife. Gasping for air, Rylie forced her arm straight out for leverage and then shoved the blade above her head as hard as she could.

Not being able to judge where she'd been thrusting, she still knew she'd hit something. The assassin screamed and the cord around her neck loosened. Just enough.

Wrenching herself from his grip, she withdrew the blade as she whipped around to face him. The assailant was holding his neck with both hands. Blood was spurting everywhere.

Horrified by what she saw, Rylie dropped the knife. When she did, the wounded man lunged toward her. His eyes were wide with pain, but the fury inside them scared her more than all the blood.

Screaming with her own rage and fear, she pushed off and shoved at his chest as hard as she could. But her blow knocked him back only momentarily. He righted himself and started for her again. But with his first step, he, too, slipped on the cola can and fell backward, hitting his head on the edge of the counter. All the air rushed out of his lungs in one big whoosh and his body spiralled to the floor like a shooting star.

Panting, gasping for air, Rylie stared down at his inert body. He wasn't moving and she was alive.

Somewhere through the blurry haze of her mind, she realized the doorbell was still ringing and now the phone was going off, too.

Numb, Rylie stumbled to the front door. Without thinking at all, she opened the locks and threw open the door.

"Rylie…darling. What the hell happened?"

"Darin." Flying into his arms, she began to cry.

She sank into him, sobbing and kissing his face.

"You're okay." His voice was steady—safe. "I've got you."

Yes, he did, she thought. For good.

But unfortunately that was her last coherent thought, as everything else around her went dark.

The woman was amazing. Darin backed out of the hotel's bedroom while Rylie headed for the shower. She swore she would be okay alone.

She'd handled a Taj Zabbar assassin. Then she'd calmly given a statement to the police. And she'd insisted she was fine when the paramedics wanted to take her to the E.R. after hearing that she'd fainted.

He guessed she could take a hot shower by herself after all that.

As for Darin, he couldn't stop shaking.

Since her condo was still a crime scene, he'd brought her here to a long-term-stay hotel where he had a reservation. When he reached the sitting room, Darin pulled out his sat phone and called Tarik. He spent a few frustrating moments trying to explain how the men had totally missed checking on Rylie's utility door and how that was the way her assailant had entered.

"You're sure she's okay?" Tarik asked again for the tenth time.

"She will be." Darin decided right then that she would be seeing the same psychologist that he'd been seeing for post-traumatic stress.

"All right. You two had better get some sleep. This time my men will not miss anything, and they have that hotel covered. You can relax."

Darin hung up but knew he would not be relaxing or sleeping.

He could have lost her for good.

Despite his and his brother's best efforts.

She could've died.

Drawing in a ragged breath, he collapsed on the sofa as tears filled his eyes and ran over to his cheeks. He snuffled. Ran a rough hand across his eyes. Then he tried to stem the tide by biting his tongue.

But nothing worked. Frustrated, he gave in to it, curled into a tight ball and cried like he never had as a child.

Rylie sneaked out of the bathroom after her shower, expecting to find Darin asleep on the king-size bed.

"Feeling better?" He sat in the dark, the only light coming in from the open bathroom door behind her.

He was magnificent. The mere sight of him reminded her that she was alive. His features were so strong. His shoulders so broad. He was vital. Vital and totally alive.

Sitting there, he looked relaxed with his shirt and shoes off. It seemed as if he'd been thinking the same thing as she had. She had been dying to feel the warmth of his arms once again. To have him surround her, keeping her safe.

"Much better. But I'm exhausted. I don't feel sleepy yet, but I'm so tired I can barely continue standing here."

"Go ahead. Climb in. Sleep will do you good." He waved at the wide stretch of clean, crisp linen, but he didn't seem to have any intention of joining her.

Dropping her towel, she hoped the sight of her naked body would induce him—seduce him. She slid between the sheets and sighed. Loudly. In her best come-hither tones.

But Darin didn't make a move.

She gave him a few moments and then said, "Aren't you coming, too?"

"I'll sit right here, making sure you're okay. You'll be able to sleep more soundly if you don't have to worry about anyone sneaking up on you."

"Darin, please." She patted the empty spot beside her. "I need you to hold me for a while. Maybe…maybe we can talk until I stop seeing that assassin in my mind."

She didn't have to ask him twice. But he came into the bed still dressed in his slacks. Instead of slipping in beside her, he stiffly placed his back against the headboard.

Rylie cuddled closer and laid her cheek against his bare chest. When she was settled, he put his arms around her.

"You're going to be safe from now on," he whispered. "Something like this will never happen again."

"You can't promise that. I know the Taj Zabbar still have a price on my head."

Darin felt good to her. So warm. She listened to the steady beat of his heart under her ear and it anchored her to the room. To life itself.

"Your whole life must change drastically from here forward. You know that."

"Yes, I know. I couldn't go back to that condo now even if I thought it was safe. I would keep seeing all that blood. I'll have to move."

"Rylie," he began again in the most somber tone she had ever heard him use. "It's more than that. Much more.

"I'm sorry I left you alone in the hospital," he confessed. "I was being an ass. But I've changed. Nearly losing you for good has changed me."

She wanted to ask how, or to put in her own opinion on his leaving. But she could tell he had a lot more to say. So she kept her mouth shut, held her breath and listened.

"I won't ever leave again. From now on I'll be your shadow."

"Oh, Darin…"

"Wait. There's more. I want you to move out of the States and come to the island of Lakkion where the Kadirs have their headquarters. We can keep you safer there."

"Hmm." She had a feeling she knew what was next, but she wanted him to take the lead. "You make a Greek island in the Mediterranean sound like a prison. What would I do there?"

"Relax. Breathe in freedom. Know you are safe."

She grinned against his skin but wasn't going to let him off the hook. "Do you know that Tarik offered me a place on his covert investigations team?"

"What? No. You can't. It's too dangerous. I'll give you a job on my…"

"Team?" she offered. It was all she could do to hold back the giddy chuckle.

He wanted her. This wasn't only about keeping her safe. But he didn't know how to say it. Rylie wasn't sure what she truly wanted and couldn't help him.

Darin took her by the shoulders and moved her back a little, letting him get a good look at her expression. "Maybe you would be safer if you changed your name. How does Rylie Kadir sound?"

"You think Kadir sounds safer than Hunt? You're crazy."

He bent his head and took her lips in one of the

wildest kisses she had ever known. She responded, reveling in the sensation of being wanted so desperately. But she wanted him, too, and her eyes were wet with tears by the time they came up for air.

"Marry me."

Gasping for air and feeling powerful, she grinned. "No."

"No? But...I thought..." His eyes welled up and her teasing mood disappeared.

She needed to take a stand for what was right. "I'll gladly move to Lakkion with you, Darin. I'll work beside you, and I'll sleep beside you. But I won't marry you."

"Why not?"

"We don't know each other well enough yet. We need to have a lot of long talks. Ask me again in six months."

He captured her lips, showing her how he felt about that. This time, the kiss was all about need. Possession.

"Just be with me, then," he finally whispered against her lips. "I'll change your mind."

With that, he flipped her over and tucked her beneath him. Showing her exactly how he would change her mind and at the same time making sure she felt safe.

Rylie squeezed her eyes shut while the two of them went off into their own world. She absorbed his strength and gave him her own.

And not too long afterward, Rylie had a vision of the future. Despite not knowing each other well, she was sure what she and Darin had between them was going to last.

Maybe forever.

Epilogue

Six months later

"I call." Tarik shoved his chips to the center of the table. "Show your cards, brother."

Darin fanned out his cards and waited while the rest of the table groaned. His inside straight beat everyone else's hands—without question.

Shakir and his two cousins scooted back from the table and stood to stretch.

"It's late and I'm busted," Shakir said. "Besides, I want to go check on that new intel Rylie found this afternoon."

Gathering the cards for another deal, Rylie glanced over at Shakir, her face contorted with concern. "You really think that list we came across of women being held for sale in Zabbaran contains a name you know?"

Shakir nodded. "Unfortunately, yes. That's what I need to find out for sure. I'll see you all in the morning."

Their cousins mumbled excuses and left the table, too. That left Rylie and him—and Tarik. Darin turned his attention to his brother and glared meaningfully.

"Oh." Tarik raised his eyebrows and was obviously fighting to keep the grin off his face. Damn him.

Yawning, Tarik drawled, "Well, I guess I'd better turn in, too."

"Wait a second, Tarik," Rylie said. "I wanted to know more about that operation we were talking about. Specifically, what did you find out after Karim finished decoding those Taj Zabbar papers Darin found in Geneva?"

Tarik stood but stayed next to the table. "For one thing, the Taj Zabbar suspected we'd been infiltrating their operation in Turkey." He grinned. "We had. But we got our man out before they ever pinned him down. What they don't know yet is that we're infiltrating many more of their operations. I've even put a couple of men straight into Taj Zabbar."

Rylie smiled at him but spoke softly. "Be careful. I know you think they're stupid. Behind the times. But they are still extremely dangerous."

Tarik reached over and patted her shoulder. "Don't worry. I wouldn't underestimate anyone with the kind of friends the Taj Zabbar has. Good night, all." He finally left the room and closed the door behind him.

"One more hand?" Darin held his breath and prayed Rylie would say yes.

She stretched, in the that ultrasexy way of hers.

"Okay. But I'm almost out of chips. What'll I use to place a bet?"

"If I win," he began casually, "you'll have to do whatever I say."

Rylie laughed and shrugged. "Oh boy. Now, what naughty things do you have in that mind of yours?"

When he only raised and lowered his eyebrows, she laughed again. "Okay. It might be fun. But if I win, you have to fix all the meals for a week."

"Deal."

She dealt the cards and he came up with three aces. He drew two more cards and found the fourth. Tarik had promised to fix the cards for him. Guess he'd been good as his word.

When the hand was over and she'd admitted he'd won easily, Rylie heaved a heavy sigh. "You win. Do I dare ask what you have in mind for me?"

He stood, moved closer and knelt at her feet.

She began to giggle. "Right here? You're sure?"

Then he pulled the jeweler's box from his pocket and her expression changed. "Oh."

"Marry me."

He opened the box and her eyes went wide. She took one look at the ten-carat diamond and began to cry.

"You don't like it." He tried to hide his disappointment. "I wanted something substantial. Like you are. I wanted something crystal clear and multifaceted. Like you. When I saw it, I was sure you'd love it, too. But you don't. We'll take it back."

Tears poured down her cheeks, making his heart ache.

He took her in his arms and patted her back, hoping to stem her tears. "The ring doesn't matter. What matters is

I love you and I think you love me. It's been six months. We've talked and talked until I think I'm talked out."

Darin had never said so much to anyone. He'd told her about feeling guilty over his mother's death. Rylie had told him about her guilt over her father. They'd cried together and vowed to keep talking for as long as they stayed together.

Now he would be sure they stayed together forever. "And I won the bet, love. You have to marry me."

Rylie reared back and stared at him through shining eyes. "Do you realize that's the first time you've ever said you love me?" She reached for the box. "Of course I want the ring, silly. You picked it out. It's perfect."

He put the ring on her finger and she started to cry harder.

"I've been trying to figure out how to ask *you*," she said through her tears. "I thought you'd changed your mind about getting married. Or that maybe you'd forgotten your promise."

"I will never forget any of it." He held her close and closed his eyes. "And I will always love you."

How amazing it was that their lives had changed so dramatically. She'd once been a grief-stricken woman who couldn't ask for help. And he had once been a detached bastard who'd needed both his ass kicked— and a big hug.

Now, after admitting they weren't perfect, they would be able to keep each other safe. Safe and loved.

Always.

* * * * *

COMING NEXT MONTH

Available July 27, 2010

ROMANTIC SUSPENSE

SRSCNM0710

REQUEST YOUR FREE BOOKS!

2 FREE NOVELS
PLUS
2 FREE GIFTS!

Sparked by Danger, Fueled by Passion.

YES! Please send me 2 FREE Silhouette® Romantic Suspense novels and my 2 FREE gifts (gifts are worth about $10). After receiving them, if I don't wish to receive any more books, I can return the shipping statement marked "cancel." If I don't cancel, I will receive 4 brand-new novels every month and be billed just $4.24 per book in the U.S. or $4.99 per book in Canada. That's a saving of 15% off the cover price! It's quite a bargain! Shipping and handling is just 50¢ per book.* I understand that accepting the 2 free books and gifts places me under no obligation to buy anything. I can always return a shipment and cancel at any time. Even if I never buy another book from Silhouette, the two free books and gifts are mine to keep forever.

240/340 SDN E5Q4

Name _____ (PLEASE PRINT)

Address _____ Apt. #

City _____ State/Prov. _____ Zip/Postal Code

Signature (if under 18, a parent or guardian must sign)

Mail to the **Silhouette Reader Service:**
IN U.S.A.: P.O. Box 1867, Buffalo, NY 14240-1867
IN CANADA: P.O. Box 609, Fort Erie, Ontario L2A 5X3

Not valid for current subscribers to Silhouette Romantic Suspense books.

Want to try two free books from another line?
Call 1-800-873-8635 or visit www.morefreebooks.com.

* Terms and prices subject to change without notice. Prices do not include applicable taxes. N.Y. residents add applicable sales tax. Canadian residents will be charged applicable provincial taxes and GST. Offer not valid in Quebec. This offer is limited to one order per household. All orders subject to approval. Credit or debit balances in a customer's account(s) may be offset by any other outstanding balance owed by or to the customer. Please allow 4 to 6 weeks for delivery. Offer available while quantities last.

Your Privacy: Silhouette is committed to protecting your privacy. Our Privacy Policy is available online at www.eHarlequin.com or upon request from the Reader Service. From time to time we make our lists of customers available to reputable third parties who may have a product or service of interest to you. If you would prefer we not share your name and address, please check here. ☐

Help us get it right—We strive for accurate, respectful and relevant communications. To clarify or modify your communication preferences, visit us at www.ReaderService.com/consumerschoice.

SRS10R

Five hunky Texas single fathers—five stories from Cathy Gillen Thacker's LONE STAR DADS *miniseries. Here's an excerpt from the latest, THE MOMMY PROPOSAL from Harlequin American Romance.*

"I hear you work miracles," Nate Hutchinson drawled. Brooke Mitchell had just stepped into his lavishly appointed office in downtown Fort Worth, Texas.

"Sometimes, I do." Brooke smiled and took the sexy financier's hand in hers, shook it briefly.

"Good." Nate looked her straight in the eye. "Because I'm in need of a home makeover—fast. The son of an old friend is coming to live with me."

She was still tingling from the feel of his warm palm. "Temporarily or permanently?"

"If all goes according to plan, I'll adopt Landry by summer's end."

Brooke had heard the founder of Nate Hutchinson Financial Services was eligible, wealthy and generous to a fault. She hadn't known he was in the market for a family, but she supposed she shouldn't be surprised. But Brooke had figured a man as successful and handsome as Nate would want one the old-fashioned way. *Not that this was any of her business...*

"So what's the child like?" she asked crisply, trying not to think how the marine-blue of Nate's dress shirt deepened the hue of his eyes.

"I don't know." Nate took a seat behind his massive antique mahogany desk. He relaxed against the smooth leather of the chair. "I've never met him."

"Yet you've invited this kid to live with you permanently?"

"It's complicated. But I'm sure it's going to be fine."

Obviously Nate Hutchinson knew as little about teenage

boys as he did about decorating. But that wasn't her problem. Finding a way to do the assignment without getting the least bit emotionally involved was.

Find out how a young boy brings Nate and Brooke together in THE MOMMY PROPOSAL, coming August 2010 from Harlequin American Romance.

MYSTERY MCF CASE FILES.

ENJOY ALL FOUR INSTALLMENTS OF THIS NEW AND INTRIGUING

BLACKPOOL MYSTERY

SERIES!

Follow a married couple, two amateur detectives who are keen to pursue clever killers who think they have gotten away with everything!

Available August 2010   Available November 2010   Available February 2011   Available May 2011

BASED ON THE BESTSELLING *RAVENHEARST* GAME FROM BIG FISH GAMES!

MCF0810